DOBRY

Every day holds a new adventure for Dobry. From harvesting his family's delicious tomatoes and peppers to listening to the exciting stories his grandfather tells, there is always something to do in Dobry's Bulgarian village—and he shares it all with Neda, the shoemaker's daughter and his best friend. And Dobry has a special talent that sets him apart. He is an artist so talented that everyone feels sure he will leave the village to seek his fortune and never return. But how could Dobry ever leave the place where his heart lives?

"There is an intimation [in the illustrations] that this is the illustrator's own story; it sounds like the story of a real boy. Readers will find him a friend."

—*Books*

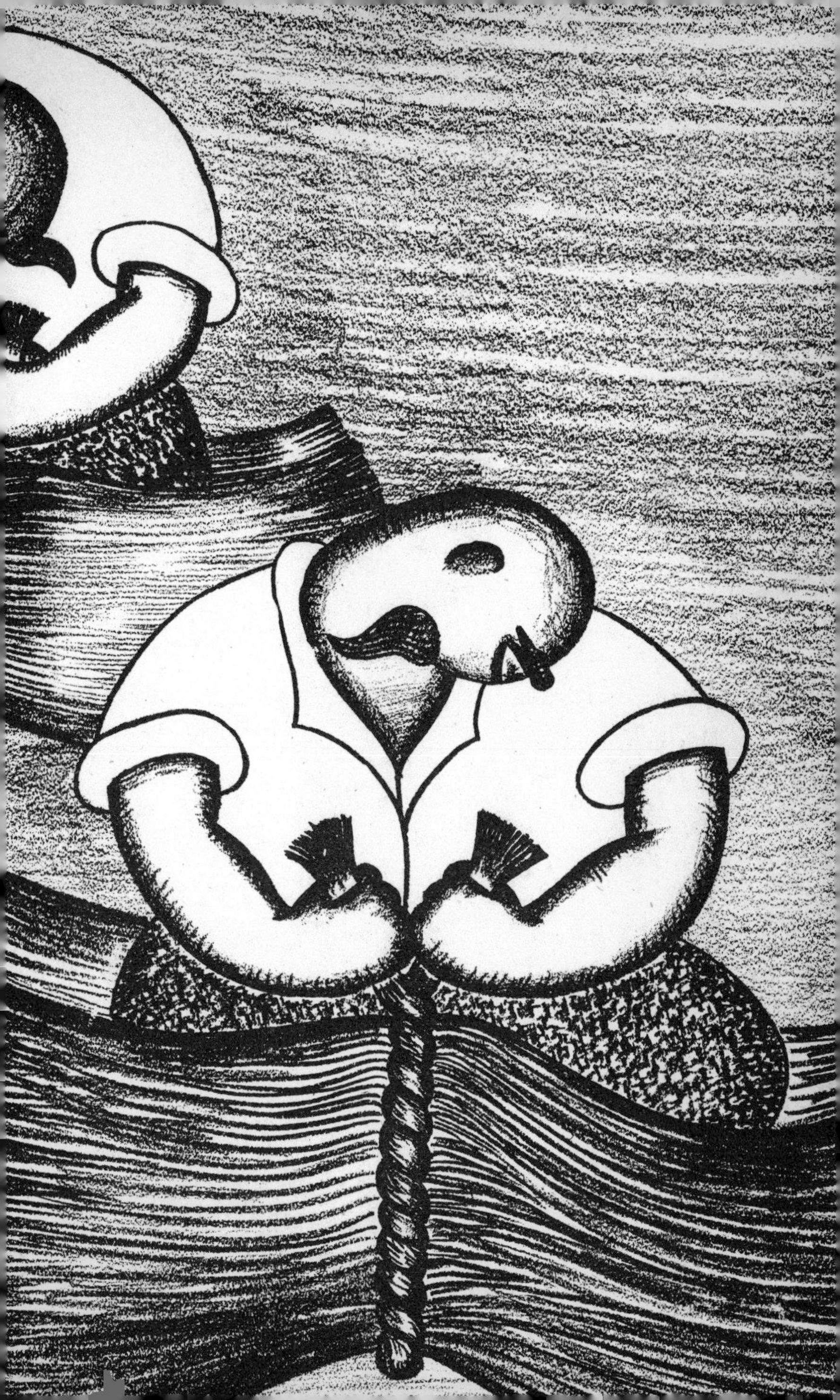

DOBRY

DOBRY

by

MONICA SHANNON

Illustrated by

Atanas Katchamakoff

PUFFIN BOOKS

HELEN M PLUM MEMORIAL LIBRARY
LOMBARD, ILLINOIS

PUFFIN BOOKS
Published by the Penguin Group
Penguin Books USA Inc., 375 Hudson Street, New York, New York 10014, U.S.A.
Penguin Books Ltd, 27 Wrights Lane, London W8 5TZ, England
Penguin Books Australia Ltd, Ringwood, Victoria, Australia
Penguin Books Canada Ltd, 10 Alcorn Avenue, Toronto, Ontario, Canada M4V 3B2
Penguin Books (N.Z.) Ltd, 182–190 Wairau Road, Auckland 10, New Zealand

Penguin Books Ltd, Registered Offices: Harmondsworth, Middlesex, England

First published in the United States of America by The Viking Press, 1934
Published in Puffin Books, 1993

3 5 7 9 10 8 6 4 2

Copyright Monica Shannon Wing, 1934
Copyright renewed © Monica Shannon Wing, 1962
All rights reserved

LIBRARY OF CONGRESS CATALOGING-IN-PUBLICATION DATA
Shannon, Monica.
Dobry / by Monica Shannon; illustrated by
Atanas Katchamakoff. p. cm.—(Puffin Newbery library)
Summary: A Bulgarian peasant boy must convince his mother that he
is destined to be a sculptor, not a farmer.
ISBN 0-14-036334-3
[1. Farm life—Fiction. 2. Bulgaria—Fiction. 3. Artists—
Fiction.] I. Katchamakoff, Atanas, 1898– ill. II. Title.
PZ7.S529Do 1993 [Fic]—dc20 92-31442

Printed in the United States of America
Set in Garamond No. 3

Except in the United States of America, this book is sold subject
to the condition that it shall not, by way of trade or otherwise,
be lent, re-sold, hired out, or otherwise circulated without the
publisher's prior consent in any form of binding or cover other than
that in which it is published and without a similar condition including
this condition being imposed on the subsequent purchaser.

3 1502 00315 5338

DOBRY

LIST OF ILLUSTRATIONS

DOBRY

ROMANIA
YUGOSLAVIA
BULGARIA
LESKOVETZ
BALKAN MOUNTAINS
SOFIA
BLACK SEA
ALBANIA
GREECE
TURKEY
CONSTANTINOPLE
ARCHIPELAGO

DOBRY ran to a window, slid back its window-panel carved with buffalo heads. "Snow! Why, it's snowing, Grandfather! The courtyard is white already." Snow was never rare in a mountain village of Bulgaria, but nobody, not even Dobry's grandfather, had seen snow coming down to hide red apples on the tree, late corn on the stalk, ripe peppers in the field, grapes on the vine. The golden-leaved poplar tree in the courtyard of Dobry's peasant home was completely hushed with snow. Wool, too, from the autumn shearing was hanging out to dry. The wool grew thicker, the thickest wool imaginable as more and more snow came down. Without making a sound, the sky itself seemed to be coming down bit by bit.

"Nobody has ever seen a happening like this one,"

Dobry's grandfather said, and followed the little boy to the window. "Snow already, even before the gypsy bear gets here! My back, my legs complain of getting in the grass and the early corn. They wanted a good rubbing before snow set in. Snow? To the devil with gypsies! They should be here with the massaging bear!"

Dobry hung out of the window as far as he could. The rickety outside stairway going down to the ground floor where their two oxen lived had a carpet of snow, immaculate, and the oxen looked up from their stalls each wearing a furry hat of new snow.

Dobry shouted, "Look! Sari and Pernik are surprised too. Look, Grandfather, they wear white fur hats like royalty!"

The grandfather leaned out. "It's true." He shook his head instead of nodding because in Bulgaria you shake your head for "yes" and nod your head for "no." "They do look like royalty," the grandfather said. He drew in his head, shivered, muttered, "You feel the first cold. Anyway, you feel it when one day is like summer and the next day like winter. Come in out of that."

Dobry pulled his head in, turned around. His hair and eyelashes had gone completely white.

"St. Nicholai, the Miracle Maker, bless us all!" The grandfather stared at Dobry. "You look just like me with all that white on you. Snow is blowing in! Close that window tight."

"Wait, wait," Dobry begged and cupping his hands he put them out for snowflakes. "Look, they are beauties," he told the grandfather. "Look at the shapes! Flowers from the sky."

The grandfather shook his head vigorously instead of saying, "Yes, yes." "Each flake is a different one. Perfect! All white flowers—little, new, and no two alike."

Dobry asked him, "And why aren't the snowflakes alike, Grandfather? Different, each one different?"

The grandfather said, "Everything is different, each leaf if you really look. There is no leaf exactly like that one in the whole world. Every stone is different. No other stone exactly like it. That is it, Dobry. God loves variety." Grandfather found it hard to say exactly what he meant. "God makes better icons than those in the church. He makes a beautiful thing and nothing else in the whole world is exactly like it. That is it, Dobry. Something for you to remember."

"Why?" Dobry asked him.

"Well, it's as good a thing to remember as anything. I never went like you do to the school but I know it. No two things are exactly alike. In odd days like these—snow comes too early, the gypsy bear too late—people study how to be all alike instead of how to be as different as they really are."

Grandfather slid back the window-panel, threw a log on the open fire, pushed it in farther with his foot, and sat himself down on the three-legged stool under the fireplace hood reaching far out into the room.

Dobry, his mother Roda, his grandfather, all of them called their fireplace a "jamal" and a jamal it really was. It stood out from the wall, tiles green, yellow, blue, glimmering in the firelight, and its big yellow chimney was stuccoed to make a picture of quail hiding in ripe grass.

Dobry squatted on the hearth. Above his head under

the jamal's hood dangled copper pots, copper kettles, and copper pans, tarnished now because the gypsy cleaner had not yet come to brighten them up for the winter. He looked at the flames, content to watch their colors, their motions, and listen to their chat, but his grandfather interrupted.

"Ours is the most beautiful jamal in the whole village," he said. "No other like it. It knows its work, too. Never smokes. Heats up the whole house instead of trying to change the weather outside. Only Maestro Kolu could have made a jamal like this one."

"Couldn't you make a jamal like this one? You could, couldn't you, Grandfather? And the blacksmith could make one too, couldn't he?"

Grandfather said very loud, "Pff! Pff! Not Pinu, the blacksmith. That fellow! Maestro Kolu is a Macedonian and almost a magician besides. He puts little pipes into a chimney the way God puts blood vessels into our bodies. Perfect! The heat goes around but stays in the house. Maestro Kolu knows the secret and that secret has been growing up for centuries. He knows how to make a jamal as no other man knows it—tiles colored up like our stony earth, the chimney a picture like one of our fields. I tell you, if Maestro Kolu lives to be five hundred years old he'll never have time enough to make the jamals people ask him to make. And——"

Realizing all of a sudden that he was roaring instead of talking, the grandfather stopped to laugh at himself. "Some day you will see Maestro Kolu, maybe, and then you will know for yourself what he is."

The old man got a pipe out from the sash winding

seven times around his middle and, his pipe filled, going, he felt around in his sash for a red pepper and gave it to Dobry to nibble. Dobry never could guess at all the things his grandfather tucked away in that broad red sash making a middle for his blue homespun suit. Pipes, coins, red peppers, cheese, bread, garlic, wooden boxes of spices to brighten up his bread in the fields, a painted flute—Dobry often saw these things come out and always asked himself, "What else may be in there?"

Dobry's mother hurried in from the kitchen fetching a bucket of water to heat in the cauldron hanging from big iron chains over the open fire. She added to the brightness the firelight made in this room of plain wooden walls and carved wooden panels—there was so much color to Roda that in the summer field bees often sought her out. Her cheeks and black eyes glowed, her white lace petticoat swirled below a sunflower-colored dress and an apron woven over with roosters just about to crow. A white kerchief topped her head and her hair danced behind her in two long braids.

"What is this?" she asked them. "A boy thinks of everything except going to bed. A big, sleepy boy and long after his supper time! A boy grows big enough to down four bowls of buttermilk at a sitting and he can't tell bedtime yet! We must be up and out before the sun is up and out tomorrow. Peppers to come in and be dried, corn to come in and be husked! When are the roads going to be cleaned up for hauling? There is too much to do now that it snows when it shouldn't. Pop yourself into bed, Dobry!"

Dobry said, "Everybody expects me to go to bed the

way bread goes into the oven. Pop! Am I bread? Mother, you should see the way Sari and Pernik go to bed. You should see it! Close one eye, eat a little more, open that eye, close the other, and eat a little more. Very slow. And Grandfather said they were good beasts fit to wear tall fur hats like royalty. Didn't you, Grandfather? You should see their hats, Mother. Snow, very new. Perfect!"

His mother said, "There it is! A boy can think of everything except going to bed. Bread, ovens, fur hats, royalty even. Go to bed!" She stooped and kissed Dobry. "The whole world taken by surprise! All these snowflakes dancing the horo outside—and this boy! Well, I must go and look after the bread. The bread is growing up now."

Dobry said, "Good-night, Grandfather," and kissed him.

The grandfather told him, "Don't forget to pray to St. Triffon about the gypsy bear, will you now? How late those gypsies are and the snow early! Ask St. Triffon to bring the gypsies soon with the massaging bear."

"Do your back and legs complain much tonight?" Dobry asked him.

"Yes, always a little. Ever since I weeded tomatoes when the fields were wet."

"Do we eat the tomatoes now, Grandfather? We always eat tomatoes after the first snow comes."

The grandfather nodded his head emphatically to say, "No, no. It's not winter yet. Tomatoes are for winter. Later snows will cover them just right. Then we'll have tomatoes, a few at a time, and a whole vineful of tomatoes for Christmas Day—the way we always do."

Dobry's grandfather alone of all the villagers knew

how to make snow take care of his tomatoes for him. He picked the tomato vines with their ripe fruits, wove them together in a weaving dense enough so that not the smallest chink was left for frost to get through. Snow covered his pyramid of tomatoes on their vines and all winter long he had only to dig down into the snow to bring up tomatoes as fresh but crisper than the morning they first ripened.

"But can't I eat some tomatoes right away?" Dobry begged. "This snow will make them crisp. You said all summer, when I helped you weed the tomatoes, you said to me, 'When snow comes you will be very happy, Dobry, for all this work. When snow comes we will both be warmed to red inside with tomatoes.' Don't you remember, Grandfather? And snowflakes are dancing a horo dance outside right now."

"Oh, yes, the snowflakes dance but without the music." The grandfather hummed and made gestures with his hands—he imitated a peasant beating a drum, playing a fiddle, blowing a pair of bagpipes. "I love the music," he cried.

Dobry jumped up, whirled about, dancing the rachanitza. Like every other Bulgarian child, he had learned the national dance when he first learned walking. The grandfather took a flute from his sash, closed his eyes, swayed his body and played the rachanitza music. Dobry danced faster and faster and Grandfather began stamping his feet.

The room was lighted up again with Dobry's mother. She called out, grabbed at them both. The flute stopped,

the dance stopped. "Now, good night!" she said crossly and turned back to the kitchen.

Happy from the music, the grandfather said, "Yes, yes, I think we had better have tomatoes now that the snow is here. Bring me in some, Dobry, when there is time. I'll be so busy getting our peppers in out of the snow. Tomatoes—we will both eat a big plateful! Nice and crisp after the snow. The first snow of the year—it is true we should celebrate. The snow comes too early, the gypsy bear too late—we need them, tomatoes to warm us to red inside. Lots of tomatoes!"

Dobry said, "Perfect!" and kissed his grandfather good-night.

Dobry lay in his bed, but excitement had him awake. The snow was all down, the moon up. A full-grown harvest moon, it stared at Dobry through the window.

"Why do you always follow me around?" Dobry asked the moon. "Everywhere I go there you come looking, looking, looking. Everything happens at once—snow comes when it shouldn't, the gypsy bear doesn't come when it should and you—you say nothing. Just follow me about, staring! How do you expect me to sleep? Nobody could sleep while you stare the way you do and say nothing. I should go for the tomatoes, anyway. Grandfather needs them to warm him to red inside and there will be little time tomorrow. Everything to do."

While he talked, Dobry got out of bed, picked up the homespun breeches he had just taken off and knotted the legs at the bottom, making twin sacks. "One to hold tomatoes enough for my grandfather, the other to hold tomatoes enough for me," he told the moon. He put on goatskin sandals and a long, belted sheepskin coat, slung the breeches like sacks over his shoulder and, calling to the moon, "Well, come on!"—ran out on and down the snow-piled stairway.

Dobry stopped at the floor below to look in on Sari and Pernik. He said to them, "What! No hats? You look just like yourselves. One eye open, one eye closed, eating away. You think of everything, don't you? Everything except going to bed!" He opened the heavy stall door, went in, patted them both and said firmly, "Good night, Sari. Good night, Pernik."

It took Dobry and the moon only a few minutes to go to the small forest of pine and fir trees separating Dobry's home from his mother's fields beyond. He could hear the happy whistle of his own breathing and his feet sounded nice in his ears as he broke through fresh snow. But in a little while the going seemed hard. Dobry stopped to pant freely on a hilltop while the moon rested too, but very far up on a cloud.

Below them the forest was deep in new snow, immaculate with the heavy snowfall. Trees had gathered to themselves all the snow they could hold; only the points of black fir trees and pines were still uncovered. They branched out like horns and made blue shadows on the freshly covered earth. Dobry could not speak to the moon now. Silence was alive here, he knew, and the moon gave it light. A radiant silence took possession of Dobry as well.

But on a sudden two owls began calling to each other, "Hoot—oo! Hoot—oo!" One of them flew low over the boy's head and he picked up an owl's feather. Then he slid down the hill, loose snow giving way behind him. ("Chasing me," he told himself.) His heart stopped thumping when he saw his mother's fields just ahead. They looked homely, familiar even in the moonlight. Walnut trees and corn-stalks Dobry knew well stood up in the snow. A very fat rabbit out to get carrots instead of tomatoes bounded across the fields, off for his hole, and Dobry noticed how dimly yellow a rabbit can look by moonlight, becoming almost a piece of it.

"Rabbits are always out when you are," Dobry told the moon. "Whenever you are following me around I have only to go outside to see rabbits going places in a big hurry. If you tried to follow a rabbit, first you would have to go very fast—hippetty hop, and besides that you would have to squeeze down a hole. With me you have only to look in through a window."

He stooped over the pyramid of tomatoes, dug down through the snow, filled up both legs of his breeches with tomatoes, slung the pack over his shoulder, called out to the moon, "Come on, moon," and ran for home. The tomatoes felt heavy enough at the start and got heavier as he ran on. But he kept going, running slower and slower down the trail his coming had broken through the new snow. Perspiration squeezed out all over him and he ate handfuls of snow to quench his thirst.

Tired out and hardly able to keep his eyes open, Dobry sat up in bed eating his share of the tomatoes, skin and all just as if they were apples, while the moon stared in at him through the window.

"There is sense to your staring now," Dobry told the moon. "Me—I should hate to just look on while somebody else ate the first tomatoes of the year. Crisp, too, juicy and really cold. Perfect!"

ROOSTERS crowed long before sunup. Dogs barked. Oxen and buffaloes snorted over their breakfasts. The church bells rang out although it was a Thursday, but instead of calling the villagers to church the bells called them to clear the trackless streets so that oxen and buffaloes might bring in out of the snow cartfuls of apples, corn, red peppers, and grapes.

Only Dobry lay abed. His grandfather was off with the other men to hurry in the fruits and vegetables, his mother kneaded bread for its second rising. She had looked in on Dobry when the first rooster crowed.

"Up, up!" Roda said. "Breakfast on the table. What could keep a boy in bed?"

Dobry opened his eyes and they looked very big, very dark and solemn to his mother. "My belly aches," he told her. "They hurt me."

"They hurt you? Who did?" his mother asked him and her voice sounded alarmed.

"The tomatoes hurt me. I went out last night with the moon to get tomatoes for myself and Grandfather. You could have had some, too, if you wanted them. We were going to celebrate this first snowstorm. But you see how it all turned out!" Dobry rolled from one side of the bed to the other in his pain.

"Lie quiet, my dear, lie quiet," Roda told him. "One batch of bread is already in the oven. Baked before long. Then I'll soon have you better."

"If only the gypsy bear would come he would have me better in no time," Dobry said.

"Poof! The bear never bothers to massage little boys. He massages only the grandfathers, great-grandfathers and people like that."

"But I—I need him," Dobry told her.

His mother pushed back his hair, rolled him up in a blanket, and put him in a chair by the open window.

"There!" she said. "Now you can see everything that goes on in the courtyard."

Dobry looked down into the courtyard full of trampled snow and lighted up by a thin sun. In the middle of the courtyard the poplar tree sagged with its snow, tips of golden leaves shining out. Like a cloud hiding sunlight, Dobry thought, a very woolly cloud newly washed and dried.

The smell of baking bread came up to him from the

courtyard stove, a table-like stove made of whitewashed stones, two roundly arched ovens on top, each with its own little roof of broken red tiles.

Roda opened one oven door, peered in—opened the other oven door, peered in. Swinging about on her heels, she smiled up at Dobry, shook her head to tell him, "Yes, yes, the bread is done." She took from the oven four huge steaming loaves, each wrapped tightly in horseradish leaves, rolled them quickly in her apron, and dashed up the outside stairway to put two hot loaves of bread at Dobry's feet, two more on his stomach.

"The new loaves are sure to cure you," Roda said and made his blanket fit him snugly again.

"Perhaps. They feel wonderful—so hot. And the smell is perfect. But just the same I wish the gypsy bear would come."

His mother said, "Poof! The hot bread is enough, plenty. And such good bread! You must hurry to be well. This bread will be full of taste when you eat it with your buttermilk. And if the gypsy bear gets here soon enough he shall have a big hunk to eat, too. The bread that made you well will be sure to make a great doctor out of him."

Roda ran down the stairway again, built up wood fires in the ovens until before long Dobry saw the openings grow redder than their little tile roofs were red. Watching the flames blink faster and faster, he began blinking himself, slower and slower, until he had blinked himself asleep.

When Dobry woke up from his nap he felt completely comfortable, his feet warm, his stomach warm, and the smell of new bread in his nose. The oven doors were still open but the fires had burned down to enormous embers.

Like the eyes of giants, Dobry thought. Two forest giants out on a winter late afternoon, making their eyes glow big so that they can see their way through the whole forest.

Feeling warm, better, he watched his mother rake out the coals, all of them, and put into the very hot ovens big fat cakes she had enriched with eggs and rolled and twisted from the bread dough until they looked like coils of rope. Roda closed the oven doors, noticed Dobry leaning out of the window, and called up to him:

"Well, how are you now, Tomato Eater?"

But before Dobry could answer his grandfather shouted out, "Hello! Hello!" at the courtyard gate.

Roda called back, "Hello! Hello there!"—as she ran to let in a big wooden cart full of red peppers pulled by Sari and Pernik. The grandfather got down, blew on his fingers, and began swinging his arms in a semicircle to keep the blood running fast. Though his cheeks were blotched red from cold, his shirt and long sheepskin coat were open at the chest, wide open to the weather.

"Hello, hello!" Dobry leaned out the window.

The grandfather peered up at him. "How are you? How are you now? I'll be up there as soon as these peppers are unloaded and stored."

DOBRY was sitting up by the living-room fire when his grandfather came in. "The peppers are all put away," he told Dobry. "Sari and Pernik watered, fed, and bedded down." He strode to the fire before he asked, "How are you, anyway? If you had waited to eat the tomatoes how well you would be now and we would have a big celebration together. Everybody is going to celebrate tonight and all day tomorrow because the harvest is in. Nothing frozen. Think of it, Dobry, nothing frozen and this is the earliest snowstorm I ever saw! But you—you ate all your tomatoes last night instead of waiting for me. Well, no matter, no matter. We learn as we go. Even at my age

I still learn as I go. And you did bring in a nice lot of tomatoes."

"And I have something else for you," Dobry said, "an owl's feather for cleaning out your pipe. I found it when I went out with the moon last night. A big white feather, speckled brown! I put it on the little table beside your bed for a surprise. Don't look at it until you wake in the morning. You won't, will you?"

"I won't look at it before sunup I promise you that. I'll wake up in the morning, stare, frown at it like this, and say to myself, 'What the devil! How strange! An owl's feather? But how did it get *here*?' And I'll feel just like a king does when I tuck it away in my sash. Very proud!"

Dobry's face lighted up. "You might tell me a story, Grandfather, to celebrate the harvest—nothing frozen. Just one story before you and mother go off to celebrate with everybody else."

His grandfather sat down and began:

"God had worked for a week, Dobry. The stars, moon, and sun were in their places and going around in more beautiful motion than wheels. The earth was made—it mountains with giant trees, its seas with giant fish. The first clouds were in the sky looking very white, very new. Perfect! The sky was the fresh morning sky, the first blue that had ever been made. God rested. But as He rested another idea came the way ideas do come when they are least expected. God said to Himself, 'I'll make people to enjoy this good earth. I'll make men very strong to match up with the mountains, the trees, the four winds and great waters.'

"Whereupon God made very big, very strong men—

giants. And before long the whole world was peopled with giants. Now, Dobry, a giant always busies himself in a quiet, slow way—a big, clumsy way. A giant will take his time and fish a whale out of the ocean for breakfast, take his time and uproot a pine tree, carrying it home on his back for kindling wood. If there was a cloud in the sky one of these giants was certain to be wearing it for a hat. And when the sun was too hot every giant sat himself down to drink a mountain pool dry.

"But the grass blades under the trees grew no taller or fatter than they do now, for after all a blade of grass is a blade of grass, and God loved its perfection in littleness. The apples and nuts on the trees grew no bigger than they do now and God loved their perfection in littleness. He could not bring himself to wish them any larger. 'They are as they are,' God said.

"Whereupon the giants complained more and more of hunger, for it took armfuls of grass to make one loaf of bread, and any giant ate ten loaves of bread at a sitting. God said, 'My people grow hungry and the grass blades, apples, and nutmeats are as they are—perfect in their littleness. I shall make a new kind of men for the earth—very small men to match up with the grass blades, the fruit, and the nutmeats.' Whereupon the earth was peopled anew, but this time its people were dwarfs, very small, neatly made to match up with earth's grass, earth's fruit, and earth's nutmeats.

"And it was to give these little people courage that God made the smaller birds—larks, tomtits, robins, the ones that have brief light songs. And God planted the paths of these little people with clovers, both white and red clovers, and sowed very small flowers all over the earth. The very small flowers that we scarcely notice, Dobry, though each one is perfect in its littleness. And God created mist to wet up these small flowers without destroying them. He made pebbles and minnows for the streams, glowworms and fireflies and crickets. God made more things than we can ever hope to see or hear for these dwarfs and said to himself, 'Now I have made for these little people, things that the clumsy eyes of a giant could not see and the clumsy ears of a giant could not hear.'

"Nevertheless, the dwarfs were not happy. The Four Winds were too big for them and scattered them as if they were leaves. The mountains were too tall for them to go over, the trees too high for them to climb. The rivers and oceans and seas were too big for them to cross. Rains made puddles that came up to their necks, snows made drifts that were icy mountains to them.

" 'My people are too small,' God thought and sighed. God looked at the earth, saw its enormous mountains and seas, giant trees and bowlders, and listened to the Four Winds, their rush of music. 'They are as they are,' God said. 'Perfect in their bigness.' Whereupon God peopled the earth anew with us middling-sized people who can climb mountains, ride on the seas, and still know the clovers, hear the songs of the robins and crickets. A middling-sized people who can love both perfection in bigness and perfection in littleness. And we are as we are, too, Dobry."

"Now tell me another story," Dobry said. "Tell me the story about the big poplar tree in the courtyard, the only poplar tree in the whole village. I love that story about the way the poplar trees got planted the day I was born, about my father and everything."

"You eat too much at once," the grandfather said, "too many tomatoes, too many stories. I'll tell you the poplar tree story before long. Not right now. Everything is good but not too much of it. The fire, it feels good, doesn't it? And you saw how it baked the bread that made you well. But too much fire in the wrong place will burn everything up. The water—good to drink, good to grow the tomatoes, good to wash in—but too much water out of place carries everything away. That is it, Dobry. Everything in the world is good, everything good in its place. You look so well, Dobry, your cheeks like two frosty apples. That reminds me! I have a present for you." He took a big, very round, very red apple from his sash, and said, "This is the pick of the orchard. Wholer and redder than any apple I ever saw."

Dobry held the apple very carefully in his two hands "Perfect!" he said.

The grandfather shook his head, "No worms, no bruises even."

Dobry's face lighted up. "I'll put it on the little table by mother's bed for a surprise," he said. "Don't say a word. When she wakes up she will wonder and wonder."

WHIRRING noise, immense and rattling noise woke Dobry up before it was light. "Kites," he thought, "millions of kites," and jumped out of bed. It did sound as if the sky were alive with the kites Bulgarian boys make whirl and rattle in the wind. But Dobry saw that all the village storks were wheeling about the sky calling to each other. "Storks!" He pulled on his clothes as he ran out and climbed onto the roof.

The mayor's storks, the blacksmith's storks, the shoemaker's storks, the coppersmith's storks, everybody's storks came together on the roof of the village church. Their feathers stood out, their wings flapped and they halloed, talked to each other, called out with as much whir and rattle to their voices as if they were run by machinery.

Snow everywhere! The roof of the village church feathered with storks! But the sun on its way up could rim only certain mountain tops with gold and turn a canyon of snow into a golden torrent, because the sky was heavy with clouds.

Dobry felt wind from the north give up to a wind softer and much warmer. The storks rose on the new wind, went up like one big dappled bird and stretched themselves for a mountain top. Reaching the peak, all the village storks flew off into a great, stormy dawn. Dobry shouted out his "Good-by!" to them all.

It began to rain as the storks disappeared, slow rain at first, a drop on Dobry's nose, a drop on his hand, and then the clouds over his head burst open. Snow began to go under his feet and Dobry got down off the roof so fast that he could not slow himself down, and he startled his grandfather by rushing in on the old man as he knelt by the hearth trying to get damp logs afire in the jamal.

"What got you up this early, Dobry? Wide awake, too. Your eyes look very bright for such a dark morning and how wet your hair is!"

"The storks went away at sunup," Dobry told him. "I heard them when they first began to talk about going. You and mother snored. They said 'Good-by' to the whole village from the roof of the church and got themselves up and off. Our mayor should have been up on his roof to say 'Good-by' for the whole village. Don't you think he should, Grandfather?"

"Storks gone already? That means an early winter for

us. I must get our wheat to the mill. Here, Dobry, you can help me on with my sash."

Dobry picked up from a stool the yards of red woolen sash his mother had woven and held one end tightly, while the old man took the other end, put it about his waist, and spun around like an enormous top until the sash was wound about his middle.

Grandfather glanced at the fire. "It burns now," he said and went to his bedroom, filling up the sash the way any man fills up his pockets of a morning.

Dobry slid back a window-panel looking down onto the village street. The eaves of his house came out very far, making a roof for the cobbled sidewalk as did the eaves of every house in the village so that in any kind of weather people could walk along under a roof. And on even the stormiest days peasants could lean out their front windows in comfort and see whatever happened. Dobry saw what was happening now and felt sorry because with this rain the roofs across the way and the locust trees that made a top for the street would be snowless before long, and his friends the storks had already gone. He was glad enough that he had seen the storks off but he knew he would miss them dreadfully. They were always amusing to watch, just like moving-pictures to him; and now the excitement of the early snow would soon be over, too.

Nobody was walking on the village sidewalk, it was too early for that. And only a boy went down the slushy road, taking six cows off to pasture. A tall boy, dreamy and slender as his father, the village coppersmith, he looked after cows because a year of this work would get him a

flute, a real flute from Sofia. The boy's sheepskin clothes kept out rain, but the cows, of course, were wet and getting wetter all the time. Dobry noticed how very spruce the cows looked and younger, too, because they went faster than usual, pelted as they were by the dripping trees. He called out to the boy:

"Hello, Asan! Your cows are running away to pasture. Hup! Hup! Hup!"

Asan looked up sleepily, then his face wakened to a smile. His father was a Pomak, a Bulgarian who had turned Mohammedan to please the Turks, the only Mohammedan in the whole village, and Asan often felt alone because of that. But the vitality in Dobry's rugged little body, his eyes beautiful with life because his spirit was awake to every moment, never failed to lift Asan up.

"If ever I catch up with these cows I'll tell them your mother needs a pitcher of cream."

"Yes, do," Dobry called back. "Our cow's going dry. Ask that cream-and-buttery-looking cow in the lead for it, won't you?" He thought to himself, "I wish I could look after cows. Asan is the first one in the whole village to take to the morning road and it must be nice to be out in faraway fields as much as he is. I wish he'd hurry and get that flute, though. Everybody expects to play it, a new big flute—the kind people play in Sofia. Everybody will wish to play the tune he knows best on it. I'll play the gypsy song, 'Na Lay.' "

No sooner had Dobry thought of the gypsy song than he began to sing it at the top of his lungs:

> "Yesterday has disappeared,
> A smoke that left your flame.
> Tomorrow? What is tomorrow?
> Tomorrow is only a name.
> Only now, this moment lives,
> A lark that lifts his wings
> Without a thought for yesterday,
> Nor for tomorrow sings.
> Na lay, na lay, na lay,
> The sun lives only for today."

"Dobry!" his mother called but could not make him hear. She put a hand on his shoulder. "I went in to wake you and here you are up—dressed, everything!" She closed the window-panel and straightened out Dobry's damp black hair. "Your grandfather is waiting for you to help him feed the chickens and the pigs. Sari and Pernik, too, they worked very hard yesterday. And breakfast will be ready soon. We are going to have the good bread that made you well. I have never seen a boy looking better than you look! I must save out part of the dough that cured you to bake up for the gypsy bear. Remind me, won't you?"

But Dobry felt sorry again. "The storks are gone, Mother, and now the snow is going, too."

"Never mind, there will be plenty of winter snow for you to play in and when the storks come back they will bring the spring with them. And a rainy day is the best kind of a day for stringing peppers. So many peppers in our fields this year! Nobody ever saw a crop bigger. We have red peppers enough for the whole village. Everybody is invited to come today and string what peppers they need for the winter. Important people will be coming. We must be ready for them."

Though it rained still harder, people began coming soon after breakfast. Women came with skirts over their heads so that not one drop of rain could stain their best dresses when they crossed a street. Men came in their holiday suits covered up with sheepskin coats. The mayor came early, bringing with him Hristu, the shoemaker, and Neda, the shoemaker's little daughter; also the blacksmith, Pinu, and his wife.

Michaelacky, the mayor, dressed like every other man in the village except that his woolen sash was much wider and woven from the pick of the autumn's shearing and his sheepskin cap was longer, a very long cap which creased down into three circles instead of having only one or two circles like the caps of other men. And white-haired Michaelacky had immense width to him, the biggest nose in the village, and lots of blood in his dark cheeks. To tell the truth, the mayor looked exactly what he was: a person of importance.

And the blacksmith, Pinu, though he was a tall, brawny man, looked no bigger or stronger than any other man in the village—every man in a mountain village of Bulgaria looks big and strong enough to be a blacksmith.

Roda served cherry sladco to all her guests. They sat on three-legged stools around the jamal fire which had only new air to warm up because the windows looking onto the village street were open to let the music of rain and the smell of rain come into the room. Grandfather brought in a tubful of red peppers at a time and got out a jug of sauerkraut juice from a cubby-hole back of the jamal. Peppers went on the strings so fast that he could do nothing at all except serve his guests and refill the pepper tub.

Dobry and Neda sat on the floor under the hood of the jamal. Her coming made the day completely a holiday for Dobry and he said to Neda, "Stringing peppers is more fun than I thought it was going to be."

Neda had blue eyes—very unusual in that dark-eyed village—and her hair was light brown instead of black, lighter brown now with fire-light on it. And because Neda was motherless the blacksmith's wife had woven her a golden homespun dress. Her father had cobbled for her, out of the skin of their last year's pig, a prettier pair of shoes than he had ever made and the coppersmith had fashioned two copper buckles for them. But the apron she wore Neda had made for herself and it was embroidered with small field poppies.

"Look how pretty she is with those blue eyes and that light hair," the blacksmith's wife whispered to Dobry's mother.

Roda shook her head meaning, "Yes, yes." "God bless that child," she said. "Neda is quicker at stringing the peppers than any of us. It's in her, nimbleness. Look at the embroidery on her apron, small and even like the feathers on an oriole."

The children were first to notice that the rain had stopped. They ran to the window, hung out, and looked at the village roofs shining like new kettle-tops, smelled the locust trees drying in the sun, watched blue patches widen in the sky and clouds humped like water buffalo striding across snowy mountain tops.

The grandfather leaned over and announced to the mayor, "Michaelacky, I am going to serve up a little of the wine made the October our Dobry was born. We must drink to the good harvest—nothing frozen."

The mayor stood up and instead of using his everyday voice used the deeper, ringing tones he kept only for state occasions:

"Let us drink to *Now*, this very moment!" he called out. "Now! The harvest is in, the storm is over!"

"Na lay! Na lay!" everyone laughed, shouted, and got on his feet to sing the old gypsy melody. And once the music got into their blood, nothing in this world could have kept these peasants from singing. They sang songs older than Macedonia, they sang their own mountain

folksongs of birth and death, of plowing, planting, and getting in the harvest. Their heads down, they sang brooding songs—songs their own great-grandfathers had made up out of heavy sorrow and oppression under Turkish rule. Flinging back their heads, they sang out their joy in liberation. And in the clear air new washed by heavy rain their powerful voices and storm of music could be heard up and down the village streets.

Asan and his father, the coppersmith, heard the singing and hurried for Dobry's home, bringing an old violin with them and a bucket of milk for Roda. Zefira, an old Mama and the best maker of bread in the whole village, came in without interrupting the singers. They merely nodded and smiled with their eyes as she found herself a stool and began stringing peppers.

A blooming girl who bound wheat faster than anybody else in the village could bind it came in with Semo, the village schoolteacher, a young man from Sofia. Semo seemed a very odd young man in this village of hardy peasants, just as one aspen tree might seem out of place in a mountain forest. He and his Wheat Binder had been walking the four miles long village promenade as engaged couples were supposed to do on a holiday and the teacher was grateful for a stool and a fire. Dobry's grandfather, playing his flute, greeted them with his eyes and put a heap of peppers in front of Semo and another heap in front of the peasant girl.

But Dobry and Neda stole out to the courtyard, let Sari and Pernik out of their stalls to take the sun, let out the chickens and the heavy pig.

"They like to get outside after the rain as much as we do," Dobry said.

"It's pretty muddy," Neda told him and looked down at her little shoes.

"Sit up on the stove then while I gather the eggs." Dobry smiled and told her, "I only gather the eggs now because I wish to give you a new egg to take home for your breakfast."

Neda sat up on the courtyard stove and Dobry put a big speckled egg in the oven.

"There it is," he said. "If you want it, it's in there."

"I think I'll leave it in the oven where it's safe," Neda said.

"Don't forget it then," Dobry told her.

"Oh, I won't."

"Guess what I am thinking about!" Dobry asked her.

"A new egg for breakfast with paprika on it."

"No. I am thinking—about storks and—about snowflakes," Dobry said very slowly. He picked up a stick, drew snowflakes in the mud, each snow crystal quite different in shape.

"Didn't you notice how the snowflakes were different, each one a different shape? Beautiful."

Neda nodded her head to say, "No, I never notice them."

Dobry said nothing but went on drawing more and more snowflakes.

"Now I'll make you some storks," he told her. He began to draw storks in the mud, boldly outlining with his stick storks on their nests, storks flying, storks just standing to look around.

"They don't look exactly like storks," Neda said. "But they do look like something alive, all alive."

"I might make you a kite," Dobry said slowly, his face puckered up with thought. "A big kite cut out like a stork with legs and everything. I should make you a kite to celebrate the harvest—nothing frozen," he muttered half to himself. He got up. Sari put her big nose against him and Dobry patted her absently.

"I'd love a kite," Neda said.

"You'll love this one," Dobry told her. "Nobody has ever seen a kite like it's going to be. The most beautiful kite! Perfect! Everybody in the village will think one of our storks got left behind."

It was cold and almost dark when the children went indoors after putting the pig, chickens, and Sari and Pernik to bed. The jamal had burned down to a pile of enormous embers and Grandfather raked the embers back from the front of the hearth until only its piping hot clay floor could be seen.

Already the women had patted sour dough out into cakes, filling the middle of each cake with plenty of cheese and sweet butter. Roda wrapped the cakes in horseradish leaves, put them on the hot clay hearth, covered them up with copper pans, and raked all the live coals back over them. Before the last pepper was strung the cakes were baked and tasted so good to Dobry and Neda that they ate three apiece and could have eaten even more with their bowls of buttermilk.

"Very good," Dobry whispered to Neda. "Dough from the same batch of bread that cured the belly-ache in me. Mother is saving out a hunk of this dough to bake up for the gypsy bear."

DOBRY and his grandfather were hanging strings of peppers up to the ceiling of their roof that reached out over the cobbled sidewalk. They stood on ladders hanging the festoons of red peppers up to dry.

Grandfather said, "This sun is warm enough but I'm not fooled by autumn sunlight. The storks know weather and took themselves off before winter set in for good. An early winter this year! And now that we have the peppers up we must take our wheat to the mill, otherwise we may have to make the trip in a blizzard or drive through tunnels of snow. The shoemaker wishes me to take his wheat in when we go. I'll use his cart and buffaloes. His cart is newer than ours and the buffaloes are not as hard worked as Sari and Pernik are."

"Neda will come, too?" Dobry asked him.

"Of course she will." His grandfather shook his head vigorously and hung up the last string of peppers. "After today you and Neda will have to spend most of your time in the school. Na lay! We enjoy ourselves now."

It was still early morning when they left the village. Grandfather used a long pole on which bells were hung to drive the big dark water-buffaloes on, because water-buffaloes move faster if there is music. The children sat atop the wheat sacks watching to see that no sack bounced off the wooden cart.

The roads had dried to enormous ruts. Dobry and Neda laughed—that is, they really *shook* with laughter as they bounced up and down, back and forth in the cart. But the buffaloes felt less happy, especially when they came to roads so deep in forest that the sun could not reach in and dry them up. Often belly deep in mud, the heavy animals went on as best they could—snorting, and lifting high their great twisted horns as they fell and struggled to find their feet again. Only the bells kept up their spirits. Without the music the tired buffaloes would have felt an enormous urge to give up the whole thing.

Through the pine trees Dobry saw mountain tops glitter so bravely with their new snow that he cried out, "Oh, but I feel happy! Look! The rain didn't take away their snow. Look, Grandfather! Look, Neda! Snow up there. Even the sun couldn't take it."

The road came out of the forest into a river meadow still very green and hot with autumn sun, except for its linden trees. Dobry shouted out, "There's Asan!" and whistled through his teeth.

"Where? Where is he?" Grandfather called back and at the same moment spied Asan where he sat cross-legged on a little hilltop, the cows feeding around him.

"Asan! Asan! Asan!" all three of them shouted. The buffaloes stopped to drink from the river, and the children tumbled off the cart as Asan came running toward them at top speed.

"We'll lunch with you on your tilltop, Asan. Come on!" the grandfather said.

The cows looked them over curiously, the way cows do, as they used the hilltop's one linden tree still wealthy with golden leaves for shade.

The children began picking up leaves from the ground, leaves that looked too bright and strange to be left there. But the leaves were hard to hold and as they picked up more, those they already had dropped back to the ground.

"Come, come!" Grandfather said impatiently. But when he saw a leaf all ruddy gold like a living coal he picked it up, put it away in his sash, and said, "You see, the autumn leaf is the most prized leaf. Most beautiful. That's the way old age should be, always, the most beautiful time of life. Look at me!" He stood very erect, his head roofed with thick white hair, his black eyes like lighted coals, autumn coloring on his cheeks. Chest up, very tall and strong, he looked down at the children.

"Ha, I am supposed to be old—but look!" He stretched out all his muscles. "Old?"

Dobry looked up at him with profound admiration and Asan found his tongue.

"And you are the greatest story teller in the whole Balkans, too!" Asan said, looking at the grandfather with the questioning wonder everybody feels when he sees a really living person who warms other people with that spark of God he always keeps burning in himself.

Grandfather took out of his sash two loaves of bread, a goat cheese, garlic, and his tall wooden salt-and-paprika box. He divided up the food, breaking the bread across his knee, and said as he did that:

"When we eat the good bread we are eating months of sunlight, weeks of rain and snow from the sky, richness out of the earth. We eat everything now, clouds even. It all becomes a part of us, sun, clouds, rain, snow, and the rich earth. We should be great, each of us radiant, full of music and full of stories. Able to run the way clouds do, able to dance like the snow and the rain. But nobody takes time to think that he eats all these things and that sun, rain, snow are all a part of himself." Grandfather lifted his eyebrows and took six tomatoes out of his sash. He laughed, "A surprise! Two for each," he said. And they ate the tomatoes just as if they were apples, adding only a little salt.

"How good this is, to have company for lunch—how good!" Asan kept saying. And he was eager about fetching them cold water from the river while they ate and drank until not a crumb of bread or a crumb of cheese was left. When they were well on their way Asan still waved from his hilltop and the cows still gazed after them.

Their road now followed the river down the mountains

to the mill town, where the river turned into a mill pond and the mountains spread out making a little valley.

Whitewashed houses and their low red roofs were bright with sun but the narrow streets were still brighter because it was market day. Grandfather had to guide the buffaloes carefully now through peasants on their way to market with squealing pigs held upside down, little black sheep bleating, roosters crowing, and donkeys carrying butter and eggs. He also had to watch out for other carts like their own piled high with corn, wheat, peppers, and drawn by buffaloes like theirs, big and dark with long necks and twisted horns. All around them peasants were bawling, "Fresh, fresh, fresh!" But above the din a gypsy could be heard calling, "Ganos! Gano—os! Gano—o—os!" as only a gypsy could call it out.

Dobry shouted, "Stop, Grandfather! Stop, stop! It's Bekir, the gypsy. Can't we get down and follow him while the wheat is being ground? We'll go on to the mill afterward and meet you there."

"Jump out! Jump out!" his grandfather shouted back. "But start on for the mill before dark!"

Dobry and Neda dodged down the street, pushing animals to left and right as they ran, and caught up with the gypsy in the middle of the market square where he sang out louder and more richly than ever, "Ganos! Gan—os! Gano—o—os!" But he greeted the children with his eyes and laughed to welcome them.

Feeling freer than they could feel in their own village, Dobry and Neda stood on each side of the gypsy, calling out, "Ganos! Gano—os! Gano—o—os!" almost as well as if they had been gypsies themselves, and other peasant children in the crowd eyed them with astonishment and envy.

Bekir's costume was made up from costumes well known in each Balkan country, so that wherever he happened to be he felt himself a part of the place. His long cap creased into three circles was, of course, Bulgarian and Bekir wore it even more daringly than a mayor. But feeling still jauntier than he looked, Bekir tucked a sunflower behind his ear to make up the difference. His white blouse had been embroidered in Roumania, his jacket braided in Yugoslavia, his trousers woven in Greece, his red sash was a gift he took for himself from Montenegro, and his tall boots were the mountain boots of Albania.

Dobry and Neda gathered armfuls of twigs and autumn leaves, and the gypsy cleared a space and made his fire, blowing little flames to big flames with his bellows. People came running from all directions, bringing copper pots, copper kettles and pans for Bekir to clean up and whiten again inside before the long winter set in and pots grew more important as appetites grew bigger with the cold.

The children first burned the kettles clean with bits of hot charcoal and ashes and worked very quickly in their excitement, while Bekir nodded saucily to the crowd and ordered Dobry and Neda about as if he were the Prince of Copperland.

"No, no! Cleaner, my little ones! Keep up the gypsy fire as you work and you will grow faster, much taller than other children grow. Put the big cauldrons on the ground, Dobry!"

When the gypsy said that, Dobry and Neda knew it

was time to take off their shoes and stockings. Bekir gave them each a mop stick to grasp tightly and Dobry jumped into one of the big cauldrons, while Neda jumped into another. Pressing the mops down, they twirled the handles and at the same time pivoted on their heels, humming, "Sis—s—s—s" like water boiling.

Dobry called out to Neda, "You have only to do this and once in a while to purr like a cat to sound exactly like water boiling. See!"

The gypsy now took on an air as if he had only to wave a mop to change all the watching peasants into enormous copper pots and copper kettles. But instead of doing that he took the cauldron Dobry had jumped out of, set it over a strong charcoal fire to dry out, and put a little alum on it. Then he melted solder on a huge puff of cotton. With a few dramatic strokes, using the puff as any artist uses a brush, Bekir painted the cauldron silver inside and made a brave gesture as if to say, "There is only one great artist in the world and that artist now stands before you!" The gypsy bowed as if every peasant had applauded him and his ears rang with the noise. He looked at the cauldron critically, his head on one side, one wicked eye closed. "But no work," he seemed to say, "could measure up to my own great dream of what the artist I am should produce."

The children longed to stay until Bekir, so like a magician, had given every pot in the mill town a new lining, but Neda, noticing that the sun was going, whispered to Dobry:

"We ought to start for the mill. Your grandfather will worry, maybe!"

"Yes, but wait a minute, just one minute. I have to speak to Bekir.

"Listen, Bekir! Something important I need to ask you. When *is* the gypsy bear coming?"

"The gypsy bear? He's two villages away now and—let me see—yes, he'll be in your village next Saturday. Expect him on Saturday."

Dobry and Neda ran along the streets of the mill town, running a race with the down-going sun. Hoping to reach the mill before the sun was entirely gone, they rushed down cobbled streets that were no more than rough stony paths between overhanging houses. Completely wet from perspiration and all out of breath, Dobry stood at the top of the hill and panted before he said,

"We're nearly there. Let's walk instead of running!"

Neda sat down on a rock, trying to catch up with her breath by breathing as loud and deeply as she could.

The last of the sun began changing every cloud in the sky into a flag. The flags stirred, blew, shaking out rarer and dimmer colors until only the mountainous horizon was outlined with a strange white-green light.

Dobry stood without the slightest movement, watching the light.

"It's the color that an egg white is before you beat it up or cook it," Neda said. "Come on, let's hurry."

"I'm through hurrying," Dobry said. "The miller never grinds our wheat until the very last because people love to hear Grandfather tell stories while their wheat is being ground. You'll see them, Neda. They sit like people without eyes, noses, hands, or feet—a new kind of people with nothing at all except ears. And Grandfather says it's only at the mill that he can really tell stories. He says that even a cow likes to give down her milk at a certain time of day, and in a certain place, and that if he couldn't tell stories at the mill it would be bad for him."

Neda sprawled over the rock. "I'm tired all over me," she said.

"Well, haven't you sense enough to stop running unless somebody tells you to stop?" Dobry asked irritably, tired out as he was from running too long.

For answer Neda stuck out her tongue and made every noise of contempt she could make with the aid of her tongue and spittle, until Dobry began showing her how to make the louder and more telling noises of derision he had invented. "This way, Neda. Try it," he urged her, and their irritation gave way to interest and enthusiasm.

"That's very good, almost perfect," Dobry said finally, and they started jumping down the hill, jumping from rock to rock.

"We're goats, goats!" Dobry shouted. "Don't touch the ground with your feet, Neda, or you'll turn into a girl again."

"I'm one of Michaelacky's black goats!" Neda shouted behind him.

Dobry said, "Oh, I'm not being a little tame goat at all. I'm a wild mountain goat with enormous horns. And lions go tame when they see me just walking around and not even jumping."

At the foot of the hill the children turned back into themselves. Neda pulled her jacket tighter as a frosty twilight deepened around them.

"We're pretty far from home, aren't we?" she said.

They took each other's hands, because Dobry, too, felt that home was too far away.

"Millions of cartwheel-turns away," he said. "But we're getting near the mill. Listen! Don't you hear the mill stream? Listen! I just hear it."

They stood in a little wood of dense beech trees and hushed their panting. Lights of the mill town blinked on a hilltop behind them, the trees made long, pointed aisles in front of them, dimmer aisles than those in a very old church. But as they trudged on, the mill stream grew from a whisper into a roar, for the children had followed the whisper of the stream as instinctively and surely as animals follow a bell.

Clambering around a bluff, they came quite suddenly upon the mill, its lighted window picking out the stream with its half-naked poplar trees, the water wheel with its churning paddles, and the big grinding stones at work.

And in spite of the headlong noisy stream, the splashing paddles and grinding stones could be heard distinctly. Dobry said:

"The stream makes a straight-down noise. But the noise of the wheel and the noise of the grinding stones are a going-around noise: swish, swish, swish, swish. It's because they are a different noise—that's why the stream can't drown them out."

"Hello," Grandfather shouted, and helped them to ford the stream. "Supper is ready. We have been waiting for you two. Here they are!" he called, and held the door open for Dobry and Neda.

There was only one lighted lamp hanging from the ceiling of the big almost bare room, and the jamal had burned down to embers piled over a turkey cooking underneath. But it seemed almost too bright and warm to the children after the frosty dark outside.

Alexandria, the miller's wife, was as round and bright-looking as a wheel and because of the fat on her she always rolled a bit when she moved.

She took off the children's jackets and creased-down woolen caps, set out basins of water for them to wash in, gave them each a fresh cake of her home-made soap, warm towels, and at the same time Alexandria sniffed deeply, smelling out the turkey lest it should be overdone.

She unconsciously made the low clucking "tur, tur, tur!" used for calling turkeys when she carefully took the longest, widest, and plumpest turkey imaginable out from under the embers. The miller rose lazily from his stool and built up the fire again with pine logs. Neda said to Dobry:

"Look, the turkey—almost as big as a pig!"

"That's the way turkeys grow at a mill," Dobry told her. "And why shouldn't they? They can eat wheat all the day long and half the night, too, if they wish."

Neda began a singsong chant from where she lay, feeling very sleepy and tired, under the hood of the jamal: "The miller is fat, his wife is fatter, but the turkey is the fattest of all."

Grandfather knocked his pipe with loud knocks against the jamal and whispered to her, "Hshush! Hshush!" Then growled under his breath, "Dobry!!!"

Dobry, who had been sitting quietly on a stool, his face glossy and all a-sting from its recent scrubbing with home-made soap and icy cold water, had grinned and held one corner of his eye away down with a finger, a gesture which means in Bulgaria, "What the devil's the difference! Everything is a joke!"

Grandfather asked them both hurriedly, hoping to change the subject, "Well, did you have a good time today? Did you catch up with the gypsy?"

Neda sat bolt upright. "We helped him. Dobry and I cleaned out two big cauldrons. You should have seen us!"

"Then you had a good time," Grandfather laughed with relief and told himself that when children get too tired, if you let them get started on a devilment, there's no stopping them. But he said to the miller:

"When children do work they don't have to do, especially away from home, they always have a good time. Isn't it so, Boris?"

The miller shook his head and laughed. Alexandria, who was dishing up her vegetables, shook all of herself and laughed. Her laugh was gayer than any bird song and as full of music.

"Your laugh is nicer than the dinner bell they have at the monastery in Turnovo," Grandfather said to her gravely, and sat down at the table.

She said to him, "You'll tell more stories tonight, won't you? Market day—the peasants stay late in town, cook their dinners in the square. On their way home they'll be stopping here to have their wheat ground."

"Oh, *tonight!* I'll tell my best stories tonight. And I'll *tell them* better than I ever told stories before in my life. Tonight I'm going to tell the story about Hadutzi-dare and the Black Arab."

The miller and his wife pressed more turkey, more corn, more buttermilk, more wild strawberry preserves, more homemade bread on Grandfather and the children, because they could think of no other way to show their excitement and happiness. Feeling that he was being too much noticed and fussed over, Grandfather said testily:

"What the devil's the matter with *you*, Dobry? Neda chatters to you and you say nothing. Never speak a word."

"That's because he knows a secret," Neda said. "Bekir told Dobry and me a secret that will surprise the whole village! You'll see!"

Dobry said, with his mouth full, "It's a surprise that will make the whole village jump."

"What is it? Well, what is it?" Grandfather asked impatiently.

But Neda went right on, "And when Dobry knows a

secret, it fills him right up, without eating even. That's why he can't talk," she said reproachfully.

"And I'm thinking about something else, too," Dobry said. "I'm going to make something wonderful."

Grandfather had the feeling of bafflement grown people often have with children. If I keep at them about the secret, he thought, they will rake up all kinds of other things to talk about. Better to let them alone.

The mill shed with its heavy tile roof had one whole side open to the stream, with the wheel and paddles and stones for grinding the wheat. The floor was hunky with piled sacks full of wheat.

"We sleep on the wheat sacks tonight," Dobry told Neda. "We always do, Grandfather and I, when we bring wheat to the mill. The wheat gives off more warmth than blankets do. Don't you think it's grand to hear the straight-down noise of the mill stream and the going-around noise of the wheel paddles and grinding stones? Splash, swish, swish, splash! I hear them separately and then just before I go to sleep they mix together into one sound, very soft, as if everything were turned into flour."

Dobry and Neda lay down on the sacks which gave more comfortably under them than beds do. The forest on hills across the stream was blotted into the night, stars glittered like icicles in a black sky. Peasants waiting for their wheat to be ground, wrapped themselves up warmly in their sheepskins and squatted around Grandfather, waiting for him to begin.

But the miller sat on a bowlder a little aloof, his eyes on the water wheel—always listening subconsciously to the grinding stones which he changed while Grandfather told the story of Hadutzi-dare and the Black Arab. Without losing a word of the story or a jump of feeling, Boris quietly lowered the stones when his ears told him from the gradual change of sound that the wheat was turning into flour.

Grandfather spoke low, but though the place was loud with water his voice had such clearness and depth that even a whisper from him could be heard.

THE STORY OF HADUTZI-DARE

"In those days, away behind us now, the Black Arab on a horse as white and swift as a mountain blizzard, conquers twenty-seven villages. Takes twenty-seven villages and the peasants in them for his own. Takes them as if they were toys. He tears the villages and the peasants in them apart like toys, to see how they are made, and what stuff is in them.

"The sun, of course, rises in the morning and makes a day. But the peasants in twenty-seven villages do not know that a day has been made. To them it is always night. Dark. Because the sun cannot change the black night in their minds and hearts to a sunlit morning.

"The village streets are empty of peasants, the markets are empty of peasants, the village fields and mountains are empty of peasants. If a peasant ventures out of his house, taking a starving cow to pasture or a pig to market, the Black Arab steals the animal and rides the peasant down, unsheaths his sword, cuts and kills.

"Peasants huddle in their houses. Speak in gray whispers, as one speaks to the dead. The hearts and minds of

all peasant men and women and children are dead, their bodies starving. All but Hadutzi-dare. Oh, that Hadutzi-dare! He has the mind of daybreak and the heart of daybreak. Dark cannot find him. He is wide awake, new, completely unafraid. His heart is a sun, his body—Hadutzi-dare is so strong in his body that he might be half man and half rock-ribbed mountain.

"This morning Hadutzi-dare wakes up on the cliff of stone he uses for a bed. He looks up at the sky, but no sun in the sky looks down at the sun which is Hadutzi-dare's heart. He sees that a black cloud has mounted a stronger white cloud and put out the sun. Hadutzi-dare sings out and stirs up the forest trees to stronger music. He shouts and an eagle answers him. Hadutzi-dare stamps his feet, the sky is his comrade, answering him with a peal of thunder.

"Whereupon Hadutzi-dare hitches his buffaloes up to his wooden cart made from the strongest black fir in the Balkans, gathers up the reins of big iron chains, made from iron Hadutzi-dare had wrenched from the earth's bowels with his own hands. He takes his iron pole, clubbed at the end and hung with iron bells. Each iron bell turns round on its axis and makes the music of planets going around in space.

"Hadutzi-dare drives through one village. Hadutzi-dare drives through another village. Hadutzi-dare drives through all twenty-seven of the villages.

"When he hears Hadutzi-dare's iron bells and iron chains, every peasant crosses himself and prays for Hadutzi-dare. But no peasant speaks and no peasant dares tiptoe to his window to look out and hope.

"Hadutzi-dare goes on as slowly as a season goes. His buffaloes plant their feet deep in earth; strong, deliberate. With his iron pole and his iron chains, Hadutzi-dare drives his buffaloes to the valley of the Black Arab, a valley with three white rivers and four mountain torrents.

"He sees the Black Arab, a cyclone of man and horse with a mad black twisting tail, whirling toward him. Hadutzi-dare roars out: 'Mountains cannot say No to me. Rivers stop to let me pass. Valleys are my servants. The darkest canyon gives me a present.'

"Hadutzi-dare feels the strong blood flowing in his body, feels the deep confident pulse of his own heart. He takes his long mustaches out of the wind, ties them together at the back of his neck, throws off his shirt, tightens up his belt, pushes his cap on his left ear. The Black Arab tries to ride him down, as a blizzard rides a man down. Hadutzi-dare claps his hands, grabs his clubbed pole with its iron bells, and roars at the Black Arab:

" 'I have my pole. The earth and my buffaloes are with me. Ho, ho, I am strong!'

"The Black Arab draws his sword just as a storm draws lightning from the sky. Hadutzi-dare jerks the iron reins and the buffaloes jump nine leagues high and nine leagues wide.

"The sword is fast: so fast that not one of you could have followed it with your eyes. No—not one of you. It cut the air as swiftly as light cuts the air."

Dobry sat bolt upright on the sacks. "No, Dobry," Grandfather said. "You would see something move in the sky—yes. But the Arab's sword is too swift, you couldn't tell what made the flash and the whine. The buffaloes are slow, but because the jumps they make are nine leagues high and nine leagues wide the Arab's sword cannot find them. And each time the buffaloes come down on their feet, they make holes in the earth, holes as deep as wells.

"The Arab's horse rears, whinnies with rage, snorts foam out from his nose, smokes at the mouth, bleeds at the bit, wheels and reaches for the buffaloes with his feet. The Black Arab turns his horse about, and again his sword whines through the air, whining for Hadutzi-dare's blood.

"Wolves gather in the forest and howl up every hair on their backs, owls wake up to shriek. Eagles leave their crags, fly at each other. The sky opens and dumps snow out of black clouds. Ice cracks up under the feet of the buffaloes, snow flies up like a blizzard from the feet of the Arabian horse.

"Hadutzi-dare might well be afraid now, but he tightens his hold on the iron reins and at once feels all the powerful stability of his buffaloes. He lets that power flow in and through his whole being. His blood becomes a strong river, his heart a pump bringing up courage from the earth. Hadutzi-dare rises in his cart, turns himself and his clubbed iron pole into a whirlwind. The iron bells on his pole clang out a doom as Hadutzi-dare clubs the Arab down from his horse, lifts the body up on his iron pole, drops the Black Arab into one of the wells his buffaloes have just made with their feet.

"And now his buffaloes are blowing at the nose, fighting for their breath. Hadutzi-dare's arms are almost pulled out of their sockets, and he has to do battle against his will with the Arabian horse because the horse is crazed by the death of his master. Covered with sweat, covered with blood, the Arabian horse insists upon finishing the battle." Grandfather spoke lower now, his voice tightened by sorrow, and ended the story in a whisper:

"Hadutzi-dare lifts the dead Arabian horse on his iron pole. The bells begin tolling as Hadutzi-dare drops the horse into one of the wells the buffaloes have made with their feet. The iron bells toll because, although the Black Arab had no love for anybody in his heart, yet the Arabian horse had loved well even that black master."

"MOTHER! The new flour! It's here!" Dobry's face was awake and his mother became completely eager as she took the sack he pushed down to her, carried it into the kitchen herself, and opened it impatiently. She ran the new flour through her fingers, testing its fineness, smelled it, took a little in her hand and put it to her lips and kissed it.

She said to Dobry, "Well, my little Sausage, our wheat fields have done well by us this year. Bread every day from flour like this!"

And immediately Dobry saw the flour as the climax to a story. "I remember it," he told himself. "It began on that very cold morning when Grandfather said it wasn't a spring day and it wasn't a winter day. An odd day that belonged just to itself. A wet day and yet it wasn't snowing exactly and it wasn't raining exactly. What came down was part rain and part snow and Grandfather plowed it under. He was plowing when our rooster first crowed and he was plowing when that big star came out."

For three days Dobry's grandfather had plowed up their wheat fields, opening the heavy earth against its will. But Dobry's mind leaped to the Saturday that he had trudged up and down the furrows helping to sow wheat in the hilly, hunked up earth. He remembered that, because at first the sheepskin bag of seeds had felt too heavy under his arm and walking seemed too hard work. Dobry's mind was electric with remembering!

"And then Grandfather said to me, 'What's the matter with you? How you should feel! Proud! What are you carrying there under your arm?'

"I said, 'The wheat seeds, heavy,' " and Dobry hunched up his shoulder as he remembered.

"And Grandfather said to me, 'No, you carry there under your arm a whole field of tall blowing wheat. A whole wheat field! Every little seed is alive, all of life in it. You are carrying all our next winter's bread!' And I felt big, strong, very proud. And Grandfather followed behind me, covering up the seeds against whatever hungry birds might happen by."

And once the fresh, unbelievably tender blades had pushed through all that earth Dobry had to get down on his knees at night with his Mother and Grandfather to beg Saint Elias, keeper of the keys that opened and closed the Heavens, to open the sky to their wheat field and let the rain come down. How anxious they all felt looking up for clouds, hoping, reaching their hearts up for rain.

A hailstorm came when the wheat blades had grown tall, full bearded. And Dobry, his mother, his grandfather had knelt down again asking the good saint to close the sky. Yet Elias, being a very old saint given to doddering about and losing his keys, had let hail lash down part of their brave, upstanding grain.

Dobry remembered long, perspiring days lived out by the river when he helped his mother toss sheaves of wheat to a mountain breeze that only the river could change into a wind. Heavy grains of wheat fell until there were golden heaps on the ground. The light chaff blew away on the wind. But Dobry thought this happened only because they sang to the wind:

"Wind, wind take these sheaves,
Golden beards and golden leaves.
Take the chaff. Oh, blow it far!
Let the grains fall where we are."

Standing up to their knees in the autumn cold of the fast-moving Yantra River, Dobry, his mother, and grandfather washed the wheat and sang to the river:

"River, river wash our wheat,
Golden beards are ripe, complete.
Washing wheat, you bless instead
Our daily bread, our daily bread."

What the river washed they put out to dry and bleach white on rugs that were woven at home and had to be carried down on their backs and spread out along the sandy beach.

Dobry remembered it all, every moment dark or bright, and taking a little of the flour in his hand he kissed it, too. Grandfather came in and put a little of the flour to his lips.

"The earth is surely ours and we belong to the earth," he said.

"I saw Bekir the gypsy, mother. Neda and I cleaned out two big pots for him. We hissed and went 'pur-r-r-r' and sounded just like water boiling, exactly."

But his mother listened to Dobry with one ear only. She was intent on mixing the first flour of the year with yeast and water, putting it into enormous wooden bowls for its first rising over night. This was more than bread-making, it was a ritual of thanksgiving and neither Dobry, nor his grandfather, nor his mother would taste a bite of the new bread until everybody who went by their house had eaten some. Tomorrow, when this bread made from the new flour of the year was baked, it would be piled into bowls outside their front door with hunks of cheese and butter in the middle of each loaf. Everybody would stop, eat, and say from his heart:

"God bless this house and give it daily bread. Bless the people who live here, bless their wheat fields with twice as many sheaves and with even thicker beards."

But Dobry had other things on his mind as well when he got into bed that night. "Tomorrow I make the kite, a big stork for Neda," he said. "Beautiful eyes, tail, everything. And it will sound the way a stork does, 'Whir-r-r, rattle!' when it goes up on the wind. She ought to love it."

Then he wondered if the mayor shouldn't be told that the gypsy bear was on the way. "Maybe Neda and I should go and tell him. No, it's a secret!" he thought. "Let them be surprised, the whole village surprised. Neda will know and I will know. That is enough."

LIGHT and color from the dawn brightened her white-washed kitchen. Yellow leaves from the courtyard's poplar tree blew in through the window and Roda worked kneading the bread made from the first flour of the year. Roosters from all over the village crowed as she kneaded and perspired, kneaded and perspired, her long braids pinned tightly back. She slapped the dough into loaves with loud, hard slaps and, making a cluster of her fingers, pressed a deep hole into the center of each loaf, praying as she did that:

"God, please bless this bread and each person who eats of it. Bad luck blow away like chaff on the wind, good luck stay with us."

Roda covered the loaves gently with a small blanket she had woven for them to keep the bread warm enough to grow bigger before it went into the oven.

Before going out to feed the family pig, their chickens and oxen, Grandfather and Dobry came into the kitchen on tiptoe, looked under the blanket to see how the bread was rising, said "Shush! Shush!" to each other and disappeared.

"How strange this is!" Dobry thought. "Everything goes on just the same: these chickens to be fed, the pig squealing for food, Sari and Pernik waiting for breakfast, water to be hauled from the well, the courtyard to be cleaned up, school most of the day—and I need to make my stork kite! I see my stork all the time, wings out, flying, feathers rustled by the wind." Then he tried to console himself as best he could: "Anyway, I like the noise these poplar leaves make when you walk through them."

The whole house smelled of fresh bread when Dobry came home from school. The last loaves were baking in the jamal and in the courtyard ovens. But he waited for nothing, not even to coax from his mother a little new loaf rich with cheese. He took an enormous piece of wrapping paper and a piece of charcoal from the jamal and drew his stork without erasing or stopping to think. A stork crudely drawn but with life in its eyes, feet, tail, feathers—all of it alive! A stork in motion and one nobody could look at and feel nothing.

Grandfather said, "Ho! It makes me want to fly. It makes me want to grow wings, lift them up, go away whenever I want to go, flap around on the church steeple and look down on you all, even the mayor. Now I know the poplar-tree story will come true! You will be a great man, Dobry, when you grow up—just as your father prophesied."

But in his curious new excitement Dobry only half heard what his grandfather was saying.

"Now you have only to cut this stork out, Dobry. Put it on sticks and I'll help you make the whistling ruffle for the neck. It will make the noise storks make; exactly the same noise. Roda, come and see the stork!" Grandfather called.

Roda came in flushed, too. She exclaimed, "Never in the world was there such good bread! Whole wheat and yet as white as beaten egg. I have a little loaf in the jamal for each of you. Smell it?"

"But look at the stork!" Grandfather roared. "Perfect! Look, it flies! And Dobry made it!"

"A real stork!" Roda said. "You made it, Dobry?"

"Let's have the bread, Mother," Dobry said. "I'm hungry, starving! So much school today."

"Now I'd love to tell you the Poplar Tree story, Dobry," Grandfather said. "Love it! Yes, give us the bread, Roda. Don't work. Come sit down. You think of nothing but work. We eat the good bread and I must tell the Poplar Tree story. We eat! Perlitca!" And Grandfather began:

THE POPLAR TREE STORY

"It happened the day you were born, Dobry, a day like this one, only right after a storm: sun everywhere, but brighter because the whole village was wet and clean. Roofs, trees, pigs, everything looked new in the sun. Every yellow leaf looked as if Bekir had just polished it.

"The storks had left early that morning, so your father said to himself, 'I must go to the mill with the late wheat, otherwise I'll have to go through a blizzard or through tunnels of snow, because winter will set in early now that our storks are gone.' He took his buffaloes—and our cart was new then—went to the mill town with the wheat sacks, knowing that when he got back you would be here.

But the buffaloes did not know that you would be here and went along slow, plodding along the way buffaloes do. Your father shook the bells on his pole every minute and sang to the buffaloes, sang out every song he knew to lift up their spirits, yet the buffaloes went slower, as if their feet were bowlders gathering moss.

"When he had filled his cart up with the new flour of the year, paid the miller his share of the wheat, and turned the buffaloes for home your father said to God, 'Dear God, was it necessary to make water buffaloes this slow? At least,' he told himself, 'they should be called stagnant-water buffaloes!' Then he broke a branch from a poplar tree growing along the mill stream, a branch stout enough to be a tree itself, and said to the buffaloes, 'I am hoarse in the throat from making songs for you, the bells are coming to pieces from so much chiming! Now!' and he switched the buffaloes on with the poplar tree branch.

"The buffaloes came into the village almost running; at least they came very fast for water buffaloes. Everybody in the village was running, too. They called out to your father:

" 'Your son is here. Alive!'

"They did that because the two babies your mother had before you came were born dead, both of them. Two others got sick and died. Naturally your father still felt anxious about you. He drove into the courtyard, jumped from the cart, and forced the stout poplar tree branch into the soil with his whole great strength. Only a little of the branch could be seen above the ground. He said, 'If this tree lives, grows, my son will live, grow big, grow very strong. He will be a great man. He will be a man with not just a spark of God in him but a whole fire!'

"And you see the tree—the only poplar tree in the whole village! It stands above every other tree, stout branches, thick leaves. There it is, Dobry—roots deep down in our soil made it great. Your father watched it grow stouter than any other poplar tree before he was killed in the war.

" 'Deep planting, roots deep in the soil, that makes for greatness,' your father said."

A DAY usually seemed a very long time to Dobry; each hour big, rounded out with wonder. And always before this when he had something as exciting as the gypsy bear to expect days were able to stretch themselves out as if Time were elastic and only snapped back into place, became much shorter, when he looked back. But now even though he expected the gypsy bear on Saturday, Time could not stretch out to its full length because Dobry was absorbed in his drawing. The hours he used up lying on his back in the poplar leaves that paved the courtyard watching the family rooster live his own life to the full seemed no longer than minutes.

Dobry drew a picture of the rooster and the rooster's proud walk. At sunup he was out on the eaves of the house making a picture of the rooster a-crow, feathers and comb raised in salute to the coming sun. Every evening he sprawled on his stomach, drawing big, rough, very crude sketches of Sari and Pernik on the stamped clay floor in front of the jamal, where he could reach for a piece of charcoal whenever he needed one. He had only to close his eyes to see the oxen gazing out from their stalls, to see the shadows on them, every muscle in their necks, flecks of light in their eyes—and he put all that into his drawings.

His mother looked down at charcoal pictures outlined on her clean floor and felt bewildered by it all. Roda had never seen anybody draw before. The village church, of course, had icons and Maestro Kolu made pictures with stucco on jamals, but nobody in the village spent his time drawing. And although Roda thought the floor did look better with oxen heads all over it, yet she said to herself, "What has come over Dobry? He thinks of nothing but making pictures. I can't imagine!" It disturbed her because Dobry had seemed a more cherished piece of herself and such a thing as making pictures would never occur to Roda. This boy for the first time in his life became a stranger to his mother. Roda said to him:

"Dobry, now you are a little peasant, but the big peasant you must grow up to be will have no time for picture making. Don't you know that? The fields are there and what are fields without a peasant to give them the energy of all his days and the thought of all his nights? These fields have been handed down over so many centuries that nobody knows whether we belong to them or they belong to us."

Dobry was stretched out near the hearth making a drawing on an enormous piece of wrapping paper of Beata, their family pig rooting among poplar leaves.

"But I am making this for Neda," he said. "Our pig! Neda will love it. I'm going to make something else for you, Mother. The big wooden bread box! I'll draw our wheat fields on that and you and Grandfather will be working away in the fields."

His mother said nothing. Her patience was only surpassed by that of Mother Nature—with whom she shared the same intentness of purpose—but a deep placidity as natural to her as breathing covered up everything in Roda. She finally told herself, "Well, children grow out of more things than their clothes. Dobry will grow out of this picture making. A boy is a shirt woven, cut out, but not made up."

"If you come in, Mother will be cooking sour-bread cakes for us," Dobry said to Neda on the way home from school, and brought her in to see his drawings. Neda stepped carefully over the oxen heads and took a long time enjoying herself in looking at the drawings.

"But I think I like the picture of Beata most. Nobody could ever know all there is to know about a pig," she said.

Dobry shook his head. "Pigs are mysterious. When a whole pig is dressed and hung up on a pole in our cellar all ready for cooking in the jamal, I often feel like going down at night to get a little of the skin for chewing. You've chewed it, haven't you? Delicious! But people say that every time the sun sets, a dressed pig gets down from his pole, goes walking around like a ghost; and if you peel off only a little of his skin he'll jump on your back and make you carry him around. I don't believe it, exactly, but if people didn't say that, I'd go down to the cellar at night and get something to chew. And pigs *are* lazy. It would be just like a pig ghost to try and ride around on your back all night, wouldn't it?"

"And maybe you could never shake off a pig ghost," Neda said.

"Oh, I could shake it off. It might take long, that's all." Dobry rolled up the picture of Beata very carefully. "I'd rather carry this home for you," he said.

Darkness came earlier now and there was very little daylight left when the children got outside. But lamps were burning in all the houses, smoke going up from every chimney so that the street itself looked cozy and the children kicked leaves before them as they went, liking not only the loud rustle, but liking even more the sense of companionship it gave them.

Neda whispered, "Nobody, not a soul in all these houses knows that the gypsy bear is coming tomorrow!"

"Nobody knows it but us!" Dobry drew out his words very slowly. "We'll have to go in the morning and announce it to the mayor, I suppose, so that everybody will be ready when the gypsies get here. Come on, let's run!"

They ran the rest of the way, sending leaves flying in all directions, and when the shoemaker opened the door to them he said, "What has happened? You're out of breath, both of you, and all your blood up in your cheeks!"

Though Neda's father still had on his leather shoemaker's apron he was roasting a big capon in his jamal and Dobry went in to enjoy the smell. The shoemaker raked more live coals over his cooking pot to hurry up the supper and said to the children, "You both wear out your shoes racing around and now that dark comes earlier I don't have too much time for making shoes, do I? Let me look at your sandals. Yes, both of you need a new pair."

"Look at Beata! She is here!" Neda held up the drawing. "You'd know it was Beata, wouldn't you, Father?"

Hristu, the shoemaker, cleaned off his hands by rubbing them together, pushed his glasses higher on his nose.

"Be-ata! Of course! Has she really gained so many pounds, Dobry? She looks so comfortable. No nerves like our pig. Her eyes almost closed: content. We will call it 'Beata, The Contented' and hang it up—where do you say? On the chimney? There!" And Hristu hung the charcoal drawing up on the plain chimney of the jamal.

"But we might put my kite up here and put Beata some place else," Neda suggested.

"The stork? Oh, no-o! A good wind came up after you both were in school. I took the big stork out to the square. You should have seen him go up on the wind! He whirred and rattled away exactly like a real stork. All the old Mamas came with their distaffs, sat themselves down in shadeless places, and watched him flying over all the village, rattling away just as if he had been left behind when our storks migrated. A stork in the village at this time of year, calling out exactly as he should! No, we won't hang the stork away up there only to get him down again each time the wind blows. Come, let's have our supper. Dobry, your mother baked us bread from the new flour of the year. Neda, set the table and make some very good Turkish coffee! Hurry, Neda, our capon is browning!"

SATURDAY'S early morning had a black mountain frost. Grandfather came out to the courtyard at the hour he always came, but this morning nothing looked usual to him. Chickens hurried around filling their crops with wheat, Beata instead of squealing for her breakfast lay completely at ease. Sari and Pernik rolled their cuds, and Dobry was burning leaves in the courtyard stove.

"But what the devil! Dobry, once you go to bed we never know where you are!"

Dobry looked up into his grandfather's eyes as if he were looking into windows full of exciting things.

"The gypsy bear is coming today, Grandfather! Bekir told me so. And I got out early—I woke our rooster up!"

"The gypsy bear? Today! No, you don't mean it!" That sleepy look of early morning left Grandfather, slanting lines in his face like the lines that rain makes disappeared, and he looked younger by five years when he ran to the kitchen window, put in his head, and roared:

"Roda, my dear, hurry up with the breakfast! The gypsy bear comes today!"

"No! Today?" Roda said. "But breakfast is ready. Our rooster crowed earlier this morning, woke me, and I never got to sleep again. Everything is ready, bowls of hot milk with plenty of chocolate. The best cakes! Come in, both of you."

At breakfast Dobry said, "The day the bear comes feels different from any other day, doesn't it, Mother?"

"Oh yes, today seems brighter, the way our house looks after a good cleaning. It's the same feeling I have when the whole house shines when guests are coming. My kitchen seems bewitched then. Garlic and onions dance on their strings, paprika is powdered fire, coffee excites itself, boiling, and pours out with more smell."

Grandfather said, "Me, I feel as if I was playing a song on my flute—and playing it just the way I wish I could play. And this morning is the first time I begin a day without going to the well for water, feeding the animals and the chickens, and cleaning up the stalls and courtyard. For the first time! Today, the first time that I can remember. But how I'll feel tonight after my massage! Perfect! I must get out my bagpipes and practice the gypsy music. Very nimble music, tra la, la la la la!"

The black frost of dawn thawed out and disappeared as quickly as mist does. It was still early sunlight and locust trees dappled the cobbled hill that Dobry and Neda climbed on their way to the mayor's house. Yet for all the warm glitter, a certain sharpness came down from snow on the mountain tops.

"The mountains wear white kerchiefs and dark pine tree dresses," said Neda. "They dress more beautifully every day than we do on holidays. Do you suppose every country in the whole world is tall with mountains like ours?"

"Of course not, Silly One! Grandfather says that when God had the earth ready He took up his sack of mountains and strode from cloud to cloud dumping out a few mountains at a time. But when he got to Bulgaria, God began to feel the weight of the sack, so He took it by its two ears, turned it upside down impatiently, like this, and shook out every mountain in it. Hurry, Neda! Our mayor is going to be surprised, and everybody has to be ready when the gypsies come."

The mayor's courtyard was black with small goats and Michaelacky stood in the middle of them, scolding the goatherd. "Goats can be black without looking as if they were in mourning for all their relatives!" he bellowed. "If you took them where you should take them, my goats would be as fat and as cheerful-looking as bishops. Take them where there are trees, leaves! You blockhead! Goats like autumn leaves even better than my stomach likes onions. Take them off! Let them stretch their necks for leaves—that will put bellies on them! Go, go!" He sent the goatherd sprawling.

Dobry and Neda had cheeks redder than peppers, eyes like the unusually large fireflies of Bulgaria.

"We came about the gypsy bear," Neda said, all out of breath.

Dobry drew himself up, looked straight into the mayor's eyes, and said with deliberation:

"The gypsies bring the bear today. Bekir told us so in the mill town. But people won't be ready for the gypsies unless they know, will they?"

The harsh angles of Michaelacky's face changed into circles and he slapped his protruding stomach.

"Good! Good! We'll ring the church bells—let everybody know. When the bagpipers play the bear and the gypsies into the village, you take your whistles and go with them, you two. For bringing the good news I'll let you help to play the bear in with your flutes." And the mayor looked a man incapable of anger, as jolly as he was big, his fat merely an accumulation of good nature.

Long before the church bells rang out, every soul in the village knew that the bear was coming. The swiftest thing on earth is news in a village, but the bells gave this special news a proper accent and said, "It is true, it is true!" as they rang.

Women pressing their husbands' Sunday clothes in readiness for the evening's horo dance heard the bells, shook their heads, "It is true, it is true!" and ironed faster. Girls out tramping the hillsides looking for berries red enough to knot in their kerchiefs heard the bells, saying, "It is true, it is true!" and satisfied themselves with berries already found instead of looking farther. Even the mayor who had seen to it that the bells were rung felt impressed and hurried over his buttermilk to the point of choking.

Dobry cried, "Give me the bread, Mother! Put it here in my sash." For Dobry, who had never worn a sash in his life, wore one of his grandfather's today, because without a sash it was impossible to be in a procession.

Roda tucked the fresh leaves away in his sash and hung an enormous ring of bread around Dobry's left arm. "The bear is sure to be hungry when he is done with the massaging," she said.

"We'll all be hungry," Grandfather said, looking greedily at the bread, took up his bagpipes, and set off with Dobry and Neda to join the other players.

GYPSIES came streaming down the mountain paths that led to the village, all of them dressed in brilliant rags, their violins polished, their carts leafy with autumn branches, and their donkeys wearing strings of blue beads. The bear, a small cinnamon bear, shuffled along unconcerned, completely aloof from everybody.

At the edge of the village the peasant musicians, with bagpipes, drums, flutes, met up with them and began immediately to play the ancient song, "Poor Borianna." The gypsies sang out:

"The King sent out his Henchman
To mount a dunghill high,
Announce: 'His majesty decrees
No man must sue and sigh,
Stand waiting for a yes or no
While girls consult a looking-glass.
Tonight each village lover
Must wed his village lass.'
But poor, poor Borianna!
Tut, tut, Oh dear! My, my!
The man who wants to wed her,
He only has one eye.
But poor, poor Borianna!
Tut, tut! My, my! Oh dear!
The man who wants to wed her,
He only has one ear.
The man who wants to wed her
Has bandy legs, his beard
Is sharp as matted nettles,
He never has it sheared.
Oh, poor, poor Borianna!
Oh dear! My, my! Tut, tut!
She doesn't wish to wed him.
How could she wish it? But
The King sent out his Henchman
To mount a dunghill high,
Announce: 'His Majesty decrees
No man must sue and sigh,
Stand waiting for a yes or no
While girls consult a looking-glass.
Tonight each village lover
Must wed his village lass.'
But poor, poor Borianna!
Tut, tut! My, my! Dear oh!
Of all the village lasses,
She had to have this beau!"

Every peasant was dressed in his finest homespun, dyed with his best and most vivid dyes. The white petticoats of the women were heavy with gold bangles. All aches and pains were forgotten, all worries mislaid in the excitement, and no villagers ever looked less in need of massaging than these did as they crowded into the village square on the heels of the gypsies and their own peasant musicians.

The mayor lay flat on the ground and the trained bear walked up and down and across him, shuffling his feet the way all bears do. Michaelacky turned over and the bear massaged him on the other side. Grandfather came next, his shaggy white head held high: a silent man full of dignity. But once the bear had massaged him he leaped up with a happy roar that startled the gypsies and set their donkeys braying.

The gypsies fiddled away at old songs until every peasant man in the village had had a massage that wiped out all thought of his summer toil and gave him the feeling that a long vacation gives to other men.

Before the sudden dark peculiar to mountains came down, the gypsies and peasants had fires going all over the square. Coffee boiled; suppers rich in garlic began to cook. But, forgetful of supper, Dobry and Neda slipped through the crowd, around fires with their smoke, across enormous shadows, by hills of bread, hills of onions and sausages, stumbling against cauldrons of soup—intent only on finding the gypsy bear.

They found him drinking from a bucket, with the old gypsy woman who had brought it sitting near by while the bear drank. Firelight played on her cotton dress, striped green and yellow, and turned it into a dress of glinting silk. Firelight played on her gaudy bracelets, her bangles and earrings, turning them into simplicity and gold.

Dobry said, his eyes on the bear, "He looks very wide for his length, doesn't he? Could I give your bear some bread?"

The old gypsy nodded and Dobry gave the bear his loaves, breaking them up into hunks.

"Let me feed him, let me feed him too!" Neda begged, and Dobry gave her the rest of the loaves.

"He must be a very old bear," Dobry said. "See, Neda, his nose! There's almost no white left on it. When a bear is young there's so much white on his nose, the white spreads out all over his face. But when he gets older more and more hair grows on his nose until when he gets completely old I suppose there's no white left on his face at all."

The gypsy woman smiled for the first time, nodded with a more friendly nod, took Dobry's hand in her own, turned it palm up, and looked into it. Then she looked into Dobry's eyes, her own eyes surprised, and rocked herself while she intoned:

> "The great wind finds resistance,
> The great river finds bowlders on its way,
> The great bird finds few comrades."

"Oh, please tell my fortune, too!" Neda cried and held out the palm of her hand.

The old gypsy took it, peered up at Neda. "Ah, ah, blue eyes!" she exclaimed and intoned slowly:

"A spring of water brings birds,
Birds sing after they drink.
Birds fertilize the ground,
Flowers spring up.
A little spring has many friends!"

What the old gypsy woman said meant nothing at all to the children, but they loved the sound of the words and the sound of her voice as she intoned them.

Dobry scratched the inner side of the bear's ear flaps for him. "Bears like it," he said. "Dogs and pigs like it, too. He must be a very happy bear—always outdoors with gypsies, going somewhere."

The old woman smiled again and nodded her head. "Listen!" she said. "The fiddles are beginning to play, 'Na lay.' Dancing will start before long."

Every gypsy, every peasant in the village square took up the song; their world rocked with it. Stars pointing down from the autumn sky might have been silver trumpets playing 'Na lay' from above:

"Only *now* this moment lives."

For four summers now Dobry had looked after the village cows to earn the money to pay Semo for whatever charcoal pencils, brushes, paints, sketch books, and canvas the schoolmaster could get him from Sofia. Asan, freed from his task of watching the cows, helped Grandfather and Roda in the fields. The coppersmith and his son were glad enough to get tomatoes, grapes, corn, and wheat in payment for Asan's work. And Asan himself had been still gladder to be at work with friendly people after a year's loneliness in distant fields.

But Dobry felt more at home in high mountain pastures of wild grass than he did either in his mother's house or in her cultivated fields. Roda was a peasant mother.

She felt that Dobry should be learning to take his father's place in the fields he would own one day. Grandfather had talked Roda into letting Dobry change places with Asan. She did not speak of it, but in her heart Roda felt certain that things were not as they should be.

When he was at home Dobry was aware of it—the disapproval in his mother's voice, the loneliness and disappointment in her heart—but away from it he could forget, and all his daylight hours were spent far away in a world of his own choosing. The only soul astir in the village and feeling very much alone, Dobry would get his cows down hilly streets in the dark, but his heart always rose high with the sun. And nobody could be more familiar with daybreak than Dobry was or better acquainted with sun moods. He knew by heart the stubborn rise of sunfire in winter, the quick dappled sunrise of spring, the summer daybreak that burned hot and smoldered for a long time, and daybreak in autumn, with its ashes and giant embers.

Those four years Dobry had spent looking after the cows had made him familiar with every turn of night and morning. At daybreak he climbed to a new world. He entered and felt completely one with a pine forest that swayed with the wind and made music greater than any music Grandfather could play on his pipes or Asan could play on his new flute from Sofia.

From his own high world Dobry often looked down on huddles of whitewashed, red-topped villages he had never been in, watched peasants in dress strange to him cultivate strange fields, or saw a monastery on a hill and its monks at work out in their fields. He climbed to a

fresh peak every day, found a mountain spring, a waterfall, a tree or rock or bird as new to him as if it had just been created.

Dobry watched orioles, rain birds, wood crows make their nests and never wondered at their skill, for that was the way he himself worked. Whatever clouds, trees, snows, waters, sun, earth, birds stirred Dobry to wonder and happiness, these he captured in charcoal or oils. His work was crude, but it always had life in it and he never stopped working.

This July morning high snow banks were melting rapidly under midsummer heat and water rushed down the mountains as Dobry climbed up. Clouds and black fir trees made a top for his new world, red earth and pine needles made a floor for his feet, bowlders and earth lumped up into tall mountains all around him. Sun bathed Dobry with salty perspiration, wind dried him off.

It was the hottest day of an unusually hot summer tense with heat. And as he climbed with the cows Dobry whistled in answer to a flock of rain birds heading upward with him.

"The clouds don't look like mischief," Dobry thought. "We do need rain but I hope it will wait for tomorrow."

Wild strawberries he had been watching for a month were ripe now in a high meadow. Neda had promised to climb up, eat lunch with Dobry, and help him pick berries enough for both their households—and he hoped no storm would keep her from coming.

The meadow topped a cliff and Dobry waited with the cows in a field below, so that he and Neda could scale the cliff together. A stream from the higher strawberry meadow tumbled over the cliff, making a waterfall and then a pool before it became a stream again dividing the field with water. Aspens trembled along this stream, wild pansies (some people call them yellow violets) and gentians looked up from the grass.

"Plenty of grass for you all," Dobry said to the cows. "But you won't eat all the flowers before Neda gets here. And I mean it! I'll see that you don't. It's lucky you can't get up to the strawberry meadow or you'd gorge yourselves with berries. Eat every one! No wonder you give the milk you do—look, the grass! Very rich."

Dobry stretched out on his back in the wild grass, with nothing to do but look up at the waterfall and the rocky cliff it tumbled over. On one side near its top was a natural stone carving, an ancient sculpture that water had made by chiseling the stone away little by little. This natural sculpture resembled a bear.

"Exactly," Dobry said. "The Gypsy Bear! Only when he was younger, more white on the nose."

He jumped up, found a big hunk of black fir wood, yanked off its twigs, moss, and bark, and began hewing a bear out of the solid block with his knife. His eyes, his cheeks became brighter than ever; glowing eyes, burning cheeks. And as he worked Dobry ran his fingers through his thick hair until it looked like a big smudge of shiny charcoal. Impatiently he rolled his sleeves higher and opened his shirt to the weather.

Now that the boy was too absorbed to notice him, an oriole he had often tried to make friends with but never could, sang on a branch close to Dobry's ear. Enormous grasshoppers hopped over Dobry's feet, hopped over his knees, hopped onto the bear he was creating. Bees hummed around his head and a bumblebee rested on the boy's shoulder before taking off on another journey.

Neda came up the rough trail in the greater heat of the day and arrived out of breath, face hot and dusty, kerchief wilted. But her yellow dress and embroidered apron stood out, freshly supported as they were by petticoats. Neda brought along her only pet, a young black goat called "Peter." One of several orphaned goats in Michaelacky's herd, the mayor had let Neda have him to bring up on a bottle.

"I had to feel my way up over the bowlders," Neda said. "But Peter came bouncing up like a ball. Don't you think he's growing? His horns are budding, too."

"Plunge your face and hands in the pool; it's good and cold. Snow water. It will make you feel as untired as Peter looks. Here," Dobry said and gave Neda a cloth from his painting kit to wipe her dripping face and hands.

"Oh, it's grand up here!" Neda cried. "And sultry down in the village. Gentians! But aren't they big ones!" Neda laughed. "And how quiet it is here! So quiet your cows looked around at me when I laughed."

"But it isn't quiet, really," Dobry said. "It makes you feel quiet—that's all. Listen! Cow bells . . . yellow hammers knocking . . . waterfall . . . bees. It isn't quiet. Listen—the cuckoo! Grandfather says the cuckoo was once a wife who talked her head off about nothing. Her husband, Kuckoo, never once heard himself think. She talked about *nothing*—just went around the house saying, 'Heavens, it's time to make the buttermilk! No, the milk isn't half warm enough yet. Kuckoo, did you hear that hen cackle? Another egg! I'll go right out and get it. Dear me, I forgot to close the door. Flies! I hate flies. Don't you hate flies, Kuckoo? My, I'm hot! Isn't it hot, though? Kuckoo, have you seen my vegetable knife? Oh, never mind. Here it is. Right here. Nobody can say I'm not clean—why, I scour everything. There, a nice clean knife! Another cackle—did you hear it, Kuckoo? Don't bother, I'll fetch the egg in myself.'

"A magician sunned himself along their courtyard wall one morning and though he was very sleepy this peasant wife kept him awake. And while he was staying awake the magician said, 'Fool of a woman!' and changed her into a bird. That's her now. Listen! She still goes around calling to her husband, 'Kuckoo! Kuckoo!' because she always wishes to tell him something. But you know that old story, Neda."

"Me?" Neda laughed. "I never heard it before in my life. I haven't any grandfather like yours. Your grandfather is as full of stories as a pine tree is full of cones. No matter which wind blows you can always pick up a story from him. But what are you making, Dobry? A bear? A bear standing out all by himself. The gypsy bear—that's who he is!"

"Exactly," Dobry said, "only more white on his nose. The gypsy bear when he was young." He shook his head and pointed out the carving the water had made on the cliff. "There he is. Perfect!"

"Yes, I see it now. The gypsy bear!" Neda cried. "But it's not as much of a bear as your gypsy bear is. He's—I think your bear is more alive. Yes, I like yours better."

"Come, let's eat," Dobry said. "It was dark when I

had breakfast. You promised to bring goat cheese. Did you bring along plenty?"

Neda shook her head for "Yes," laughed, and repeated her laughter.

"I can't help laughing," she said. "Guess what Semo told me this morning! He came in to order shoes for his baby because—just think of it!—their baby walked yesterday. Semo told me that in other countries people nod their heads for 'Yes' and shake their heads for 'No.' Isn't that funny?"

They laughed together and Dobry said, "But don't other countries have bells? Bells always shake their heads to mean 'Yes.' " He wagged his head from side to side like a bell and ding-donged his voice: "Yes, time for church, time for church. Come in, come in!" He wagged his head faster. "Yes, hurry up, hurry up! The bride is dressed at last, at last!" Dobry moved his head very slowly as far to one side and then the other as he could. "Somebody died, somebody died. Come in, come in! You see, bells shake their heads and always do mean 'Yes.' "

He began feeding bread and cheese to the little goat. "Tell me, do you wish more bread and cheese?" he asked Peter. "Watch him, watch him, Neda! Peter shakes his head too for 'Yes.' People in other countries must be mixed up. But look, the clouds! What do you see, Neda?"

"Just clouds," Neda said and laughed.

"Oh, no," Dobry cried. "Look, the oxen plowing, leveling off mountain tops. I never saw so many clouds here. It's going to storm, Neda. Thunder clouds! Hurry!"

They scrambled quickly to the little meadow where wild strawberries were ripe, but Peter was there ahead of them and found himself in the middle of a cloud that hung low over the strawberry meadow. Its dense white fog went swirling around the little goat and he climbed to a bowlder, staying there càutiously while Neda and Dobry picked wet strawberries as fast as their cold wet fingers would let them.

"Don't range around in this cloud," Dobry told her. "Just pick all you find in one place."

The storm broke with thunder and lightning when they were halfway home.

"We'll have to jump along the way Peter does if we are going to get home dry," Dobry said. "But everybody will be glad of this rain. The wheat is dry—it rustles. How slow these cows are! And I don't dare hurry them, because of the milk. Whoop! We're almost down!"

They saw the village below them lying in a rift of sunlight.

"There's Mother and Grandfather still weeding tomatoes," Dobry cried. "And Asan out in the wheat field!"

DOWN in the fields it was sultry. Heat waves made a glare of light over corn and wheat. Hot, sulphur-like dust covered the tomato vines. The Grandfather and Roda had been at work for six hours, hoeing weeds out of the tomato fields. Roda began to complain, but she complained neither of the heat nor of her own weariness. "A strange boy helping with the corn!" she said.

"And Dobry off looking after other people's cows! A little boy who makes kites and pictures to astonish the village—that is one thing. But why should a big strapping boy like Dobry keep it up once the surprise is over? Dobry cares more for a charcoal pencil than he does for our plow. And what will it lead to? What will it lead to for him? Our fields are here. Bigger and richer than any other fields belonging to the village. If Dobry wanted to be a lawyer instead of working here with us that would be an easier life and a finer life, too, than ours. If he wanted to study in the Street of Lawyers in Turnovo I'd work the fields all by myself, if necessary, and pay for the schooling. I have seen boys in Turnovo going up and down the street with their books. Happy! Important! Those boys will have easy lives, everything they wish. And people will look up to them, too. But an artist! Bah! What is an artist? Poor, no food maybe, ragged clothes instead of good homespun. And we are decent people."

Grandfather said, "But, Roda, people are not all the same, any more than the vegetables, fruits, trees and animals are all the same. A fox lives one way; the buck another way. Both have different needs. A pine tree will die where a poplar tree will grow. Grapes need sun; celery needs shade and more water. Some plants need to be moved; other plants die if you move them. There it is, Roda. To the devil with 'easier'! What seems an easier life to you would seem a harder one to Dobry. He needs to draw, to paint, and Dobry is going to be a great man just as his father said he would be.

"I know, I understand," Grandfather said more kindly as he looked into Roda's troubled eyes and saw the tired look on her hot face. "The fields are here and Dobry is a boy, very big. Strong for his age. But after all, Roda, he is taking care of the village cows—our cow along with the rest and they are in fine shape. Everybody says, 'Look, our cows!' What Balkan village has cows fat as ours, giving the butter our cows give? No mountain pasture is too high for Dobry to find. He goes up mountains the way a goat does it. Sure of himself and quick. Dobry loves to find meadows thicker in wild grass, places higher up than our cows ever grazed. Come, what is the matter with you, Roda? For four years now I have listened to you complain and never could think what to say. I felt it very strong. Feeling choked me. But I could say nothing. Now all at once I tell you. What a relief!" Grandfather rested, held the hoe in his two big hands, put his chin down on the handle, and slacked his body.

"Yesterday at the corn husking you looked like a girl, Roda. And I saw Hristu tossing ears of corn to you just like a boy in love for the first time. Well, Hristu would make you a good husband. He is a hard worker for a shoemaker and rich enough. He made me these shoes for the Feast of John the Baptist and look, not perfect but they still last. Yes, he does his work well. He should make you a good husband. I would think nothing of the corn tossing yesterday if Hristu hadn't made me that pair of shoes for a birthday present. For the first time in my life I get a pair of shoes from Hristu on my birthday. There it is, Roda!"

Dobry's mother laughed with more of mockery than amusement. "I'll never marry. Never marry Hristu nor any other man. My husband still lives in my boy. Dobry takes up all the ground in my heart. I wish only to be a good mother and to keep our fields the most fertile fields in the village. They have always been the best fields in the village and as long as I live they always will be."

Grandfather said, "But look, Roda, when you are not complaining out loud about Dobry you are complaining in your heart. But if a boy is something, it doesn't matter what kind of work he chooses. If the boy is strong, live and good yeast, the work he chooses will rise, become great, nourish everybody. Dobry has guts—and brains. If he makes mistakes he will get out of them. I find my tongue about this today. For the first time in four years! And I know it! Bring a boy up to use his hands and brain and heart, leave his guts in him and then let him alone!"

Roda, discouraged, rested on her hoe, looked thoughtfully at the sky, looked thoughtfully at the mountains. "The storm may break any moment," she said. "It's storming in the mountains now. I hope Dobry and Neda have started down. It was clear when Neda left to get strawberries and I thought we would all have supper by the river tonight. I cooked up that old rooster. There they are now! Just starting down the trail. Can't you see Peter, jumping down away ahead of them? They'll come in wet, soaking!"

"At last the good rain! I got a drop," Grandfather cried. "Maybe I'd better make up a small fire in the jamal? Come on, Asan!" he bellowed. "We're going in. Bring some wood in with you—Dobry and Neda and Peter will need to dry out."

SUMMER was almost over—no more showers or warm dusks. It was that drab time of year before frost and sharp air fire the trees and bushes with color. And today was especially gray without any drama of light and shadow going on. A windless morning in the river pasture, its dusty linden trees had no stir of life. Bees were not out and if any birds were around, they had no songs and kept out of sight. The Yantra river was low now, slow moving. And the cows were more intent on freeing themselves from swarms of flies than on filling themselves with the scorched grasses.

Dobry had started to hew out Neda's little goat, and Peter had half emerged from a block of wood, a simple horned little figure, poised for a jump. But Dobry found it impossible to finish the carving because the chisel was as dull as he himself felt.

Instead of working, the boy sat cross-legged, watching life on an ant hill. The hill's cone-like top was thatched with the chaff ants throw out after threshing their harvest of seeds and grasses. Caravans were still arriving at the ant village, bringing in loads of wild aster seeds and crumbs from the breakfast Dobry had eaten on the river bank. Enormous loads! Each ant carried in proportion to its size a load heavy enough to crush a stout young donkey.

"Ants are queer little peasants," Dobry thought. "Silent, work all the time, and never have any fun!" He shook his head and said to them:

"But you should be celebrating. All this chaff! Why, you've had a fatter harvest than any Bulgarian village will have."

He told himself, "I like bees much better than I do ants. I love bees. Bees make something new and beautiful out of whatever they bring in. Something nobody else but a bee could make. And bees hum as if they were humming dreams of fields that were more fun, honeycombs that were more fun, and a magic honey that would turn their humming into clear out and out songs."

Dobry wished himself home in the village today, because the walnuts were ripe and after all the nuts that could be made to fall by shaking and throwing sticks at the trees had been gathered, the village boys were allowed to climb the very old trees and keep whatever nuts they found at the top. And Dobry loved climbing around in the old walnut trees, wider than houses at the top, shuttered with leaves, hospitable to every wind and bird.

Besides all that, each peasant boy counted his nuts and grew in importance as his nuts grew in number. One autumn Dobry had gathered together a hoard of a thousand walnuts by climbing out on dizzy branches where most boys feared to climb. He sprang up as he thought of the walnut harvest; then threw himself impatiently on the ground, closed his eyes, and listened to the only sound there was—a loud croaking of frogs along the river bank. To Dobry's ears the frogs seemed to be croaking "Wal-nuts! wal-nut! wal-nuts!" And with all his might he wished himself out in a village orchard with Grandfather, Roda, Asan, and more especially with Neda, beating nuts down from trees.

And home was a pleasanter place for Dobry now because a change had come over his mother. Not that Roda had become convinced that Grandfather was right and Dobry was doing as he should do. Day and night Roda had pondered every word Grandfather had said to her in the tomato field. She respected his words as much as she respected the Grandfather's profound sincerity, and told herself:

"He finds this idea of Dobry leaving the fields to become an artist completely wise and I find it completely foolish. There it is!" Months of thinking it over had left Roda without any answer to this problem, and she still waited for a solution. She could only hope that something outside of themselves would decide between the two of them.

"We'll know in good time," she told herself at last and went about her work again—happy, relaxed and as completely sure of herself as any mother stork who without thinking gets herself and her brood off before travel becomes too dangerous, and back again in time to lose no moment of spring.

And although Roda said nothing about his work, one way or the other, yet Dobry felt happier at home. Home was a more spacious place now, provided with an air of release. But exactly what it was he felt, Dobry could no more have put into words than he could have told why to him life—whether dark with mystery or lighted up by beauty—always felt as if more wonderful things were about to happen.

Lying with his eyes closed, listening to husky frog voices, Dobry did not see the cart and buffaloes that came along the road from the mill town until he heard creeping wheels and the slow deep sound of buffalo feet. He sat up, jumped to his feet, and shouted out a friendly "Hello!" although he had never before seen the driver.

A man dressed as a Bulgarian never dresses—a man dressed all in white homespun, his costume completed by a cap of white astrakhan, got down from the cart. He was as tall as any man Dobry knew, but built up in a different way. Less thickness to him and yet he looked powerful. A man just old enough to have wisdom and youth—both showing in his eyes, lighting them—and his long horse-like face was creased by humor.

"Hello!" he said and looked curiously at Dobry. "I'm Kolu, the jamal maker."

Dobry reached for his hand. "You made our jamal,"

he cried. "All my life Grandfather has been telling me stories about you. He always told me I ought to see for myself what you are."

Maestro Kolu laughed. "And that's the only jamal I ever made in your village. Any man would travel far to hear your grandfather tell stories. I knew when I was putting the jamal up that no better stories would ever be told around a fire than those your grandfather tells. How is he?"

"He's feeling his strength these days. When deep snow comes he's going to enter the snow-melting game. I'm Dobry."

"Yes, the father's name. When I was building your jamal, your father thought only of having a son—a boy, very strong, with deep roots like a tree. Well, you look that. If you don't stop, you're going to be even bigger than your father or grandfather. An ox of a boy!"

Dobry said, his face alight as it usually was, "Yes, but I'm more alive than an ox is. The ox is a slow coach. I don't feel that way. When I wake up, I'm awake—that's all. All of me awake!"

Maestro Kolu laughed with Dobry. They laughed at nothing in particular but only out of pleasure, a tribute to the spirit of the moment. Then Dobry said, "You hear the frogs? Only a moment ago they croaked, 'Walnuts! Wal-nuts!' Now they are saying, 'Kolu! Kolu!' Very plain, isn't it?"

They both laughed again.

"But what are you doing . . . carving?" Maestro Kolu asked. His voice rose in surprise. He stooped, looked closely at the carving of Neda's goat. "But it's very good. Strong and looks honest. I could never do that—never. Make a goat like that, muscles all ready for the jump—never."

"But I know the goat," Dobry said. "Neda's goat. You remember our shoemaker? This is a present for Neda, his daughter. Very blue eyes—but blue. And hair, not wavy but very shiny for brown. I make this for her. But I like the goat, Peter, too—like him very much. He grows big horns now and how he can jump. Peter can take any mountain in ten steps. You should see it!"

Maestro Kolu said, "In Macedonia we say, 'When a boy loves a girl he sees even her family pig wearing a halo and only heavy with dignity.' "

Dobry shook his head gravely but Maestro Kolu was again intent on the carving and asked him:

"Why don't you work with clay?"

"I work with what I have," Dobry told him.

"But you have it—clay. Surely. Not here, but a little farther on where that creek runs down the hill and into the river—lots of clay. I got clay there for your jamal and very good clay, too. Come along! I am on my way there for a load now to do some repair work at one of the monasteries. Come on, get in!"

Maestro Kolu drove the buffaloes on with his clanging pole of bells and Dobry noticed that the sun had come out. Lizards scuttled for good seats atop rocks. A covey of quail crossed the road in front of the slow cart, their top-knots trembling with excitement, chittering themselves and setting all the quail in roadside bushes achitter too.

Kolu left his cart at the river's turning and he and

Dobry climbed the hillside, following the creek only a little way up.

"There it is—clay," Maestro Kolu said. "A bank of clay."

They shoveled out enough to fill up the cart, loaded it in, and then Kolu said:

"Now I'll show you how to work the clay up with water, squeeze out the extra moisture, and make it ready for modeling."

And he took great pains to show Dobry exactly how the work should be done. "There!" he said, and he handed the boy a big lump of the clay. "Now you can model—"

"Right from the earth," Dobry interrupted and reached impatiently for the clay. "Oh, I'll love it! I'll love to make people and animals out of earth!" He worked the clay with his hand, felt it give under his fingers. "I make you first," he cried. "Stay the way you are, don't move around!"

And Dobry went to work, his lump of clay on a bowlder before him. He used a pointed stick for a tool, shook it once at Kolu, and said to him:

"Tomorrow, I ask my mother for one of our long wooden spoons. The handle is just what I need for this work. Soon though, I'll make tools for myself."

He made Maestro Kolu's head, white astrakhan cap, face lighted from the inside and creased well by all the humors of life, while the man sat on a rock by the creek, glad enough to rest and empty his mind of everything except what the present moment offered.

"There—it is you!" Dobry exclaimed, after he had

worked away for more than an hour. "I saw for myself what you are." And excitedly he pushed back his hair with long fingers. "All of you there, and right out of the earth!"

"But it's very good!" Maestro Kolu said, looking at the head in amazement. "Very good!" and he embraced Dobry. "You should leave the village, go away, study!" he exclaimed. He looked at the bust again. "Very good," he said.

"Grandfather will want to see you. Come home with me for supper?"

"No, I'm afraid I can't," the man said, as if he were trying to think of a way to change his plans and go along with Dobry. "You see, they expect me back at the monastery tonight, and early tomorrow I set to work on repairs, now that I have my clay." He glanced up at the sky. "Just time to get back before dark. But take the bust to your grandfather, Dobry. Then he'll see how well you know me. As if you had known me all your life. Take the bust to him—a present from us both. It will tell him everything."

"All right," Dobry said. "I'll put it up on the jamal you built for us and Grandfather will out-do himself telling stories. I know he will."

They laughed and were both laughing from excitement and pleasure until they had to say good-by.

THE evening after his day in the river pasture with Maestro Kolu, Dobry and his grandfather talked so long after supper that Roda, who sat with them under the jamal's hood, finally put her knitting away and said:

"You'll never be done talking—you two. I'm going to bed. Good-night, and don't forget to cover the fire." She took up her lamp and left them.

"I have everything I need now—everything," Dobry told his grandfather. "I have clay. Everything! When school opens I think I'll give up herding cows . . . have time to make people and animals out of the clay. And time to help you right here."

Grandfather said, "Oh, you'll have plenty of time, time

for everything. Not much work to do in winter. Courtyard work, wood to chop, wood and water to be hauled. Nothing! You'll have plenty of time to work with your clay . . . plenty of time. You don't have to learn a book by heart the way Asan does. Semo tells me you do all right without all that study. But if Asan needs to learn books by heart, he needs to—that's all." Grandfather knocked his pipe against the jamal and filled it up again. He looked up at the bust of Maestro Kolu, laughed, and said, "I nearly offered you a pipeful, Kolu." He smoked for a long time before he took the pipe from his mouth and went on talking.

"Semo thinks you ought to make yourself a great artist, Dobry. I think so myself. This head of Maestro Kolu now—it is Kolu. All of him. Maestro Kolu is here—that's all. And you saw for yourself exactly what he's like. Yes, I think you ought to work to be a great artist. I don't know what your mother thinks. Roda says nothing."

Dobry said, "I don't know what Mother thinks either. But she doesn't fret any more the way she used to. Hums to herself like a bee and works very slow. You know the way she does—works in a beautiful slow way."

Grandfather said, "Yes, Roda works all the time. But she never seems to be working too hard. Never seems tired any more than the earth seems tired. I'd give up the cows if I were you, Dobry. Cows give us the milk and the butter—yes. But you have to bother about cows, all the time. A pig just stays at home and grows. But a cow has to travel around and be milked at a certain time night and morning. Nobody can look after one cow even, and take a day off. You can get away from pigs and chickens:

put out their feed, go away on market day, take your flour to the mill, dance on a Feast Day—forget about them. But you can't forget about a cow! Not for one day even."

"But I love to draw cows," Dobry said. "You know that big white heifer? I drew her when she went to sleep after a long hot climb. Her muscles were looser. I know every peak and hollow in a cow, Grandfather, every hump and what she does with it. Right away I'm going to model cows. I can't wait to do animals and birds in clay. Animals talk with their bodies. Tails go up or down, ears cock or flatten back. Hair on the back rises. Muscles go loose or snap tighter. And you've seen a bird in love spread all his feathers out in the sun, haven't you?"

Grandfather said, "And no animal is too bothered with himself, bothered about what to do with himself. Animals belong to the earth. That grace of God we pray for in the church—that must be what the animals have already. This baby of Semo's now. Already that boy is too bothered about himself—never at his best any more. We're greedier than animals are, too—much greedier. I don't know what's the matter with us." To console himself Grandfather got down his flute, played "Poor, poor Borianna," and kept time by stamping his feet.

But long before school opened, Dobry had modeled other things besides cows. Bekir came to resilver the insides of all the copper cooking pots for winter use, and Dobry could not help sculpturing the gypsy. To capture Bekir's own fire and mockery and dance of spirit gave Dobry the adventure and excitement that capturing a leopard alive would give to another boy. Dobry did

Michaelacky in his three-times-circled sheepskin cap and made the mayor look as pompous as he always felt but never dared to be. He modeled the gypsy bear from life, and the old gypsy fortune teller who looked after the bear came more alive when she saw her bear growing out of a big lump of clay.

"Oh, I love to work with the clay," Dobry told her, responding to her unaccustomed friendliness. "I love it. It gives under my fingers and does anything I wish it to do. I'd like to model you."

"Not now, not now," she muttered, and peered at Dobry with those secretive eyes of hers that were always smileless. "Not now, some day in another place—a foreign city—you will make me alive again in the clay. Not now. You'll remember me exactly. You're not the one to forget. Nobody forgets me altogether. Nobody, and you—"

"I'll never forget you—I won't forget a line of your face!" Dobry interrupted.

Weeks later he finished hewing out the jumping goat he had begun in the river pasture and modeled Peter again in clay, a quick sketch full of life. It happened on an October Saturday brilliant not only with frost-made colors but with frost itself, when Neda and Peter lunched with Dobry on the creek where Maestro Kolu had found the clay.

While Dobry and Neda lunched, Peter filled himself with autumn leaves, and the good food and wine-like air brought up his spirits. Peter held himself more proudly now, as if leaves had been created only for his pleasure and food.

Using a tall flat-topped bowlder to work on, Dobry

had no sooner finished the wood carving of Peter than he began to do the little goat in clay. Working with swift, assured fingers, he said to Neda:

"I can always work better when you are with me. You do something to living, Neda. You set a match to a person's life and it flames up. It would be nothing but another cold day if you weren't here."

"But this is a beautiful cold day," Neda said.

"Yes, that's what I said. When you're here, Neda, any day is beautiful, even if it's raw like today and all the leaves are dead and wet on the ground." And Dobry had the figure done so quickly that he felt himself as breathless as if he and Peter had made the jump together.

"We have Peter twice, three times," Neda said. "A Peter that eats autumn leaves and two Peters that eat nothing."

"Which of the two that eat nothing would you like to have?" Dobry asked her. "I'll keep the other one."

"Oh, I don't know, I love them both," Neda said. "I love all three of them," and she pulled at the real Peter's goatee.

"I'd keep the wooden one, if I were you," Dobry told her. "Why not? It's dark wood, black—and might be Peter's shadow jumping at the same time with him. I think you ought to have Peter's shadow and let me keep this one made out of clay."

Neda laughed up at him and took the wooden goat. "Now you'll never be able to make me anything I'll love as much as I love this," she said.

"Oh, you don't know," Dobry cried, "I'm going to make something later on. But I won't talk about it. Not to anybody—not to you either. So don't ask me about it. Everybody in the village will come to see it. Nobody could keep them away." Seeing her eyes astir with curiosity and questions, Dobry laughed and began hurriedly:

"A long time ago when Michaelacky was a boy, he had a goat, a very young goat like Peter, who got separated from his shadow. It happened here in this very place, only it happened on midsummer's day. The goat's name was Andrino. I suppose it was the short for Alexandrino, but I don't know for sure. Anyway, he was jumping down this hill when his shadow got caught on that pine tree, stayed there, and Andrino went on without it. Being very thirsty, he stopped to drink from the creek, then ran on as fast as he could run and caught up with the other goats who were heading down the road with Michaelacky's goatherd.

"But when Andrino caught up with them the goats took one look at him, flattened their ears, lifted their hair, and trembled. They trembled and ran faster than any goats had ever run before. Andrino couldn't imagine what was wrong. He didn't have any desire to hurry, saw no reason why he should, and as the other goats were already out of sight, Andrino stood wondering what had got into them. Troubled, uneasy, he naturally looked behind him. No shadow? What, no shadow! He wondered when and where he had lost his shadow. 'No shadow, that's queer! But it must be around somewhere!' Andrino told himself. He looked around and saw the shadow of this rock, the shadow of that tree. 'But where on earth is my shadow?' Andrino asked.

"And while he was asking himself that, Andrino noticed a shadow moving across that hill over there. A shadow just big enough to be his and it belonged to nothing that he could see. But the shadow kept moving and Andrino moved after it stealthily. 'I'll catch it,' he told himself. Still trying to catch up with the shadow and then pounce on it, Andrino happened to glance up at the sky and saw a cloud looking much like himself, small, young, gray, scraggly haired, horned, and moving along right over the shadow. Andrino stared.

"A little man who had been watching, a very amused little man, got down from that stone where Peter is standing now, cracked his fingers, whistled to get Andrino's attention, and said to him, 'Wait, wait!' Then the little man sat right down on the shadow and began humming a song, a song like the patter of a little fire, the sound of a breeze in a bush, the noise of a trickle of water, a pebble slipping into a pool, the splash of a raindrop. And before the little man was done humming, a shower had started and ended. The briefest shower you ever saw, with only a few drops of rain. But the cloud had disappeared, changed into rain, and Andrino now had the cloud shadow for his own.

"Andrino walked up to the little man; the little man laughed and patted Andrino. Andrino hurried off with his new shadow. He was much quicker, now that he had a cloud's shadow, and before Michaelacky's goats reached the village Andrino caught up with the herd. There never was a goat who could jump and run as fast as Andrino could jump and run after all this happened. And I'm certain, Neda, that Peter is Andrino's only descendant. Don't you feel it yourself?"

WINTER settled down with deeper snows than usual. By early December the village streets were frozen tunnels of snow packed high and tight, arched, reinforced with planks, and open to the sky at certain places.

Dobry loved this high icy winter, and often told himself:

"Snow is the most beautiful silence in the world. And in winter we are more like ourselves. Lots of blood!"

In winter these peasants had hot blood in their cheeks and hands, livelier eyes, fingers like sausages, and more color to their clothes. Dobry raced other boys down snow tunnels instead of lagging to school as he did in September. Village dance had more bounce to it; peasants spread their bodies, jumped in the air, twirled themselves. Music burned. And sleep at night was empty of dreams, deeper than the snow and more refreshing.

Home had hotter jamal fires now, lusty smells of pork and garlic cooking. Bread was always hot, tomatoes cold from the snow, and people sat longer to talk.

Grandfather was feeling his strength. He said to everybody, "This snow of ours—magnificent! The fields will be well watered next summer. Nothing to worry about now. And the Snow-Melting Games have more importance this year. Nobody ever saw a deeper winter."

He and Dobry chopped, sawed, and hauled wood; not only for their own use but wood enough for the coppersmith, the blacksmith, shoemaker, and village priest. Grandfather and Dobry were busier than they had thought to be, this winter's immense cold having surprised everybody.

They chopped and sawed in the pine forest that separated their house from their fields, thinning out the forest where it needed thinning, sawing up fallen logs and bringing them in on a sledge pulled by Sari and Pernik. Whenever the snows packed down and turned to ice on top, they took the sledge to more distant forests and worked there. Each Saturday Dobry worked all day with his grandfather. First out in the morning, they were on their way home with a load of wood when other peasants sat at table finishing their evening meal. And of course Dobry had no time to work with his clay, but when Grandfather stopped work to rest in the forest, the boy often modeled him in snow.

Grandfather, intent on making himself fit and hard

for the Snow-Melting Games, went capless, coatless—homespun shirt open to the weather, his chest showing as much blood as his ruddy face and the sweaty hair on his chest frozen stiff with icicles. These icicles clinked all the time he was at work on the timber.

He told Dobry, "I have to win the Snow-Melting Games. This year I have to. We'll never have snow deeper than this—never. It means something to win—a winter like this one, the world closed by snow. Na lay! Anybody who wishes to do it may win next winter and it won't gall me. But now—a winter like this. I have to win—that's all!"

"I think you're fit to win," Dobry said. "Nobody else but me has chopped and sawed and hauled as much wood as you have this winter. And I'm too young to enter the games."

"Thanks to Saint Triffon! If you were twenty-one or better, Dobry, you would break our snow-melting record and make the rest of us look foolish. Right now you are the huskiest human in any Balkan village. I know it. If you were older nobody would have the ghost of a chance."

Dobry laughed. "I envy you those icicles on your chest," he said.

The Snow-Melting Games were played in the village Square. No peasant was too old or too sick to come out and watch them. Everybody was there—old Mamas wide with petticoats, babies wrapped tight like caterpillars or in cocoons of wool, girls in red and yellow homespun, bangled, and housewives with brilliant aprons over sober dresses. So cold that the nostrils stuck together and people had to keep opening their noses with their fingers—yet the day seemed warm enough to these peasants. And the feeble winter sun made a fiercer glare on their snow than the heat glare of any summer day.

Village men were divided into older and younger peasants. And Grandfather was the eldest among the older men.

"Yet, I think he'll win," Dobry told Neda. "Grandfather's got lots of blood and it's bound to be thick and rich and quick. Bound to be."

"But Pinu is a blacksmith, Michaelacky is fatter, and both of them are younger. Everybody is younger than your grandfather," Neda fretted.

"Stop talking, both of you, and pray to Saint Triffon," Roda admonished them.

Roda, Dobry, and Neda huddled together near the troop of musicians which was headed by Asan because Asan's flute was the only flute in the village that was not homemade.

Michaelacky blew a whistle and the men—stoutly fortified by a meal of sausages, garlic, a loaf of bread apiece, sauerkraut and wine—lay down atop the high snow. Capless, coatless, shirts wide open to the icy sky, a score of peasants lay there—to find out who could first melt the snow under him with the heat and weight of his body.

When snow began to melt under Grandfather, Neda pressed her hand against her mouth and whispered to Dobry, "Oh, he must win! But the others are all younger. Oh, I don't know—I can't tell which of them is going down fastest. I'm too excited to tell. I feel like a clock going so fast it can't tell the time."

"Hush," Roda whispered. "Hush, I'm praying to Saint Triffon."

"Grandfather, Grandfather!" Dobry roared and jumped into the air. "Look! Grandfather, he's winning. I knew you'd win," he shouted. "Grandfather, you're winning, I tell you. Winning."

And it was true. Grandfather was the first among the older men to disappear between high banks of snow.

Dobry rammed his way through a bellowing crowd packing itself in around Grandfather, hoisted the winner up on to his shoulders, and carried Grandfather home.

Asan—violent with excitement—took the big heads of his musicians for drums, beat on them with his flute and shouted, "Play, play!"

The musicians closed in at Dobry's heels, playing the march their ancestors had played when they first bore down upon Bulgaria and took these mountains for their own. The younger winner and all the contestants followed them down snow tunnels, marching in Grandfather's honor.

Every man who could, pressed to the jamal to thaw out his clinking icicles before drinking Grandfather's health. All day long Grandfather's health was drunk by peasants who came and went, some of them walking miles for that purpose. And certainly his health seemed worthy of the tribute.

But Dobry envied the men their icicles and whispered to Asan, "I wish I were a MAN, full grown. I'll be proud the day I can stride in here, clinking at the chest. It's a noise I love even better than the noise of sledge bells on our oxen."

Roda and Zefira—the old Mama famous for her baking—took out of the ovens loaf after loaf of bread well centered with cheese and butter. They gave each peasant a loaf of bread to break across his knee and eat with pork cut from the family pig, dressed at home and hanging from his pole in the cellar, ready to jump down and ride the back of anyone who disturbed him at night. Dobry served up the wine.

The window shutters were flung open and at the turn of day the room's wooden walls reflected a glorious light, the last of the sun from off snow. And because peasants repeat any important remark again and again and again without changing a word or a tone, Grandfather got tired of hearing body strength praised and after chewing his own thoughts as an ox chews its cud, he told the Story of the Betrothal Feast.

THE STORY OF THE BETROTHAL FEAST

"A Balkan man had two sons—Pinenik and Firnik. Both were strong, but Firnik was stronger than any man had ever been. Both sons were handsome, but Pinenik was handsomer than any man had ever been. The father owned more mountains than he needed, but no fields. And his sons had to work harder than any sons ever worked. Firnik did not feel the work. The hardest work could not tire him—but it could tire Pinenik. Yet Pinenik worked on, tired or not tired, until the job he and Firnik had started was done as it should be done.

"Firnik never knew what it was to be tired and never imagined that Pinenik knew. As for Pinenik, he always kept his ache, his fatigue, to himself and worked right on.

"The mountains they owned were not high, the trees were not thick, nor the grass tall. Rocks and bowlders took up most of the earth. Pinenik and Firnik took care of their father's goats and worked to clear their mountains of bowlders and rock. They loosened rocks, bowlders and carried them down while their goats fed. And a certain man who owned the rich level land below hired them to fence his field with the huge bowlders that no two men other than Pinenik and Firnik could have brought down.

"The rich man's fields were vineyards and fields of sunflowers raised for their seed. The land was rich, its vineyards and sunflowers were rich, and their owner was the richest man in the Balkans.

"This rich man had one daughter and no sons. The girl was called Nina after a Russian grandmother they had in the family once upon a time. Nina had the kind of wisdom that a bird has when it builds a nest no storm can shake down, the wisdom a dog has when it fasts and licks a wound, the wisdom a buffalo has when no matter where you leave her, she finds her way home. Nina had good sense and good looks. But her father thought her very wise and very beautiful.

"Pinenik and Firnik knew nothing of her wisdom and cared less, but they both felt that Nina was like sunlight—necessary and beautiful. When seeds and fruit were ripe they watched Nina harvesting the grapes, gathering up sunflowers, and both of them loved her.

"Nina's father said to her, 'Harvest time already, and I should be arranging your betrothal, because when winter sets in and work slacks up we can prepare a wedding feast worthy a daughter of these fields and vineyards. January and February are the wedding months and your betrothal should happen before frost. You need neither land nor money. You have both. So I shall not look for a rich husband nor a land-owning husband for you. Pinenik and Firnik have nothing except rocks and goats, but they are rich in strength. And I wish you to marry Firnik, the stronger of the two. Both have asked for you.'

" 'I'll be glad to marry one of them,' Nina said. 'But on one condition. Father, will you leave it to me to decide which of the two is stronger? Will you leave it to me completely—not meddle at all?'

"The father promised not to meddle, because he loved feats of strength and he loved his daughter and liked to have her wisdom displayed.

" 'Are you going to have Pinenik and Firnik turn the threshing stone instead of having our oxen do it? They could turn the threshing stone—those two hunkies! And you could marry the one whose strength stayed with him.'

" 'There you go meddling,' Nina said. 'And you promised——'

" 'All right, all right. Do as you please and I'll ask no questions.'

"Nina decided to go away with her father, but before she went she sent for Pinenik and Firnik and said to them:

" 'We shall return in three days. In the meantime you must neither eat nor drink. When my father and I return on the evening of the third day, we shall break our fasts together. But we'll break our fasts lightly, as a fast should be broken, and there will be no other guests. After we have eaten, I shall decide which one of you to marry.

" 'Father and I will return tired from our journey, but you'll find a bowl of sauerkraut in the kitchen, a small young turkey hanging up behind the door, sausages for the sauerkraut, and wood enough to cook everything. Here is the key to the house. Make everything ready, won't you? I'll send a man on ahead of us in three days' time with fruits and nuts and raisins and sweetmeats, because when we break our fast we shall be eating a betrothal feast. Father and I will bring wine—and a gypsy musician or two, with wine for the heart and head.'

"Pinenik and Firnik ate nothing, drank nothing, and for two nights slept out on the hillside with their goats. On the third day they opened the big house, took the turkey down from its hook, made it ready, built up a fire in the jamal, and put the turkey to bake under hot ashes and the sausages to cook in sauerkraut.

"They were very hungry and the whole house smelled of nothing but food.

" 'We need more wood,' Pinenik said. 'There is only wood enough for the baking. Frost tonight, and when Nina and her father come in they will be cold as well as hungry. We must go to the forest and fetch wood for the fire of hospitality, so that the whole evening will be warm.'

" 'All right,' Firnik said. 'Let's go, then.'

"They set off up the mountain and for the first time in all his life, Firnik felt tired.

" 'But what is wrong with me?' he asked, stopped felling wood, and threw himself on the ground. 'I ache all over. You will have to finish this alone, Pinenik, and carry the wood down. I am used up—I can do nothing. I never felt like this before in my life.'

"Pinenik felled the wood, carried it down, and if the brothers were hungry before, they were twice as hungry now that they had climbed and felled logs out in the mountain frost.

"The turkey was ready, the sausages cooked in their sauerkraut, and the smell of all three filled the young men's noses, but could not fill stomachs empty of everything but a lust for food.

" 'We hunger beyond endurance,' Firnik said. He filled one big spoon with gravy and another with sauerkraut and lifted them to his mouth, when a knock thundered on the door. Firnik dropped the spoons.

" 'Thank God they've come,' he cried. But it was a man with two baskets instead. The man handed in the small baskets full of nuts and fruits. Pinenik and Firnik had never before seen nuts or fruits like these. There were pineapples, citrons, nectarines, bananas and nuts strange to them, almonds and pecans. Fruits and nuts we see pictured in our grandchildren's school books but never taste.

"Pinenik set the baskets one at each end of the table. 'But we need something for the middle,' he said. 'This is a betrothal feast—we should have dran berries on the table. I'll go and cut down some mountain berries, Firnik. You watch the turkey that it doesn't burn.'

"Pinenik went out and Firnik turned the fowl and thought to himself, 'I'll just taste it to see if it's done.' He tasted the turkey, both white meat and dark, helped himself to sauerkraut and sausage, tried the new fruits and nuts. 'Well, everything tastes wonderful,' he said to himself. 'I never knew food could taste as wonderful as this food does.'

"Pinenik came in with the branches, Nina and her father and the musicians at his heels. 'Here we all are,' he called. 'Firnik, they're here!'

"But Firnik did not answer. He sprawled fast asleep with his mouth open wide though his stomach was full. Everything was gone—baskets and kettles empty. There was only Firnik to show for all the food that had been there, and Firnik was fast asleep.

" 'Now which of the two do you think the stronger?' Nina asked her father. 'Pinenik or Firnik? Which?'

"Nina's father was hungry and tired and raw with annoyance. 'Don't ask me foolish questions!' he cried. And Nina and Pinenik were betrothed, though their betrothal feast was only a dish of buttermilk and bread."

When Grandfather had done Hristu asked him, "Is that a very old story? I never heard it before."

Grandfather said, "No, it's a very new story. I made it up just now. Very new things and very old things are much alike. Everything is a circle. Both ends meet. There is nothing much older or more wrinkled-looking than a baby just born."

Neda said, "Dobry does that, too. Makes up a story while you listen," and she went to work boiling Turkish coffee, very creamy and bubbly on top, for everybody. The coffee was drunk with enthusiastic noises, and each guest belched to show his appreciation, a politeness borrowed from the Turks—and borrowed customs are never returned.

THE intense cold changed to a thaw and the villagers were able to open their snow tunnels into roads before Christmas. Then a quick freeze left the snow dry with a hard icy crust.

Because she was motherless, Neda and her shoemaker father always spent Christmas Eve at Dobry's home. Roda being maternal enough for two peasant women, had years ago made Neda's coming a habit.

Their supper on Christmas Eve was eaten earlier than usual. At twilight they sat down to the simplest meal imaginable, because the forty-day fast in preparation for the Christmas feast was never broken until after midnight mass. A suckling pig roasted under hot ashes in the jamal, Christmas breads were browning in the kitchen oven, the whole house smelled of temptation—yet supper tonight was only boiled-up fruits the family had harvested and dried. Fruit soup, they called it, and ate this Christmas Eve soup with bread, torn from a special loaf Roda had baked with a very old silver coin in the middle, the Christ Child's gift to the finder—a benediction.

Hristu crumbled up piece after piece of bread, impatient for the good-luck piece, but Dobry, eating a hunk of the bread, bit on the lucky old coin. "I nearly swallowed my good luck and my blessing!" he cried. He polished his luck on his blouse, showed it to Neda as if the world had no other coin like this one, and put the lucky blessing away in his sash.

Grandfather said to him, "Last year I got the Christmas coin, and you saw me—I won the Snow-Melting Game! And I still feel myself as lucky as a stork." He laughed. "Just having me here should bring luck to the house." He shook his head at Dobry. "Good Luck!" he roared.

But Hristu's face sagged and he thought, "No, Roda will never marry me. I'm a good-enough shoemaker, but I have no luck." He said out loud, "I never get the lucky coin—never. Not once in my life!"

Neda put her hand on his arm. "I know," she said. But Grandfather interrupted her sympathy and told the shoemaker:

"You are always too anxious, Hristu. Every Christmas Eve you take a hunk of bread, crumble it, take another hunk of bread, crumble it without eating. You are too anxious. And a too anxious person bites his own tongue, sticks his finger in his own eye, trips himself up, and misses his luck altogether. If you hold a wish too tight it can't fly, any more than a stork can fly if you hold him tight. Just enjoy your bread and some day, without knowing how, you'll bite right into luck, Hristu—the way Dobry did just now."

Dark came long before they had done talking and laughing at table. "Time to go out to the animals," Dobry said, getting up and lighting a candle for each one to take along. For on Christmas Eve, between night and morning, every Bulgarian peasant takes up a lighted candle, goes out, wakes up each family animal, and says to him or her:

"The Child is born and blesses you tonight."

The head of the family takes with him a small earthen pot of incense, holds it under the nose of cow, pig, buffalo, ox, and lets each animal have a sniff. Dobry had often climbed the tallest pine in his mother's forest on Christmas Eve and watched candles all over the village going to and back from the barns and pens. But tonight his mind and spirit were both too absorbed in the dream he had mentioned to Neda—a dream alive in him but not yet sculptured.

After Sari and Pernik, the family pig and chickens, had been awakened and told, Neda left with her father to wake up Peter and the buffaloes, let them know that it was Christmas Eve, stroke them, thank them, and give them their blessing and sniff of incense.

"I'll come and get you for midnight mass. I'll come early," Dobry told Neda before she left.

And because anticipation breeds impatience, they set off too early for midnight mass, each carrying a lighted candle.

Their village church topped a hill and on the way up Dobry stopped climbing, and said to Neda:

"I like to be outside when the chimes ring, don't you? Bells sound dull, don't mean anything much once you're in the church."

Above them windows of the big low church lighted up, candle by candle, as altar boys hurried about inside. When all its candles burned, the village church became a symbol of Light, a star at the top of a hill. And below Dobry and Neda the village bobbed with candles, because every peasant—except the Pomak coppersmiths, father and son—was on his way to midnight mass.

Stars looked dimmer, much higher than usual. The moon, cloud muffled, could have been a reflection of the lighted church and the stars only reflections of the lighted candles bobbing now on every side of Dobry and Neda.

"Don't you wish we could believe in the Christmas bird the way we used to believe?" Neda questioned him. "Don't you remember? We used to put big sheets of paper out under our eaves, wake up on Christmas morning, run out barefooted to find our paper piled high with raisins and nuts and little Christmas breads. All dropped down by the Christmas bird."

Dobry said, "An enormous white bird! Flying down from the North. Son of a Wind bird and a giant Snow bird. I never believe in him on any night in the year except on Christmas Eve. I believe in any beautiful thing tonight. That's why I know the Christmas bird will come flying over the village before morning, a gunny sack of nuts and raisins in his beak. If the north sky opened now —and it might—the Christmas bird would fly straight over our heads on his way down to the village. But if he did fly down over our heads the Christmas bird couldn't make me jump. Tonight is a wonder. Nothing less could startle me."

Chimes rang out and Grandfather, Roda, and Hristu climbed the hill and pushed on with the crowd of people roaring out greetings to each other before they stamped into the church. Only Dobry and Neda waited outside until the bells stopped ringing.

Everybody stood through the long Byzantine ritual, but not stiffly. To these peasants their church was the hearth of God and they made themselves at home, moved about, nodded, spoke quietly to each other, or called out Christmas greetings with their eyes and their wide smiles. Dobry pulled down a corner of his sash and whispered to Neda:

"Look, my good luck and my blessing. That means you love me. Now I don't have to ask you, 'Neda, do you love me?' Perfect!"

Neda said, "But look what you've done! If you show your lucky piece in a church don't you know it loses everything—luck, benediction, everything—becomes just a coin again. Didn't you know that? And if you call me a liar in church that will be worse for you."

"But I can wait until after church." Dobry laughed, held down the corner of one eye with his finger and then lost himself in the music.

Husky male voices sang the Christmas canon of Saint John Damascene, greatest poet of the Eastern Church. Without an instrument of any kind, peasants stood at each side of the sanctuary's front and chanted in answer to each other, every man expressing his quickened feelings, his child-like wonder.

And to Dobry it all seemed as old, as mysterious as the night outside did with its symbols of God. He said no prayers in words but his mind and his heart seemed to be on fire. Longing to do perfectly what he hoped to do grew into a desire strong enough to shake him and set his blood pounding. The priest in golden vestments and tall black hat, altar boys, their white banded by Mary's blue, seemed to Dobry like people in a dream and his own dream seemed real and urgent.

It was snowing when he came out of the church, surprised to find himself alone, not realizing that the others had left before him.

Neda had hurried off with Roda, intent on helping her prepare the Feast of Sparrows. But they found Grandfather home before them, keeping up the jamal fire which roasted their suckling pig. Dobry had saved out the biggest log he had felled that winter, rolled it into the jamal for Christmas Eve. Grandfather kicked the log now and got more fire out of it, while Hristu took charge of the roasted pig, watching to see that it kept hot without burning.

Dobry came home alone in the fresh snowstorm. The night was quiet—a hush of wonder possessed it and the locust trees were in blossom now with snow. The only one to come home covered with snow, Dobry's sheepskin cap, coat, boots of sheepkin had fleece again, all of them completely woolly with snow.

After midnight mass they broke their forty-day fast lightly. Nothing could be touched until little dried sparrows, soaked and broiled, were eaten. These were sparrows from the wheat fields that had known the growing of wheat and how the earth and its peasants worked together to produce a loaf of bread. The birds had been killed weeks before and hung to dry under the eaves of all village houses in readiness for Christmas Eve.

"Now we eat our sparrows," Grandfather cried.

They all sat under the jamal's hood, warmed as much by excitement as by the fire, because a sparrow eaten on Christmas Eve is supposed to put music in the soul of a peasant and make him feel that he has wings.

Grandfather finished his sparrow. "There—I knew it," he shouted. "The music is coming up in me already!" And he began to sing before he could get the flute out from his sash. But when the others sang, Grandfather contented himself with playing the flute while he thought, "It's better to keep quiet and feel the spirit moving in me."

Roda and Dobry and Neda and Hristu sang the Byzantine chants heard everywhere in the village on Christmas Eve and repeated their favorite Christmas song:

"The Day-star of the Day-star!
And we on earth who lay
In death-shade and in darkness
Have found a world of Light
For, soothly, of a virgin
Is born the Lord of Light."

The village rose very late on Christmas morning, a clear sharp morning with new snow on top the old. Only Dobry got up with the tardy winter sun. He went noiselessly, crept down the rickety outside stairway, fed and watered Sari and Pernik, fed and watered their new Beata and the chickens, cleaned out manure and old straw from pens and stable.

That done, Dobry stood a rough big charcoal sketch against the poplar tree, a naked tree now except for its snow. He massed and packed all the snow he could in a corner of the courtyard, until it piled high above his head, a small mountain of snow, immaculate, glittering with crystals of ice. Standing on a short ladder, he cut out an open stable and with great slow tenderness made the manger and the Holy Child, Mary and Joseph. Only youth could have brought the freshness Dobry brought to his Nativity, and only a primitive genius, Indian or a peasant like Dobry, could have modeled these figures with strength, assurance, sincerity—untaught in any school.

His Mary, his Joseph and Holy Child were peasants, Joseph a kindly, humorous peasant resembling Dobry's grandfather. Mary was Neda, not a beautiful Mary, but a girl strong and luminous with youth. And the child might have been any village baby looking for the abundant breasts of his peasant mother.

For the two oxen of Bethlehem, Dobry modeled his own everyday Sari and Pernik. He intended to make the ass next, because he had done it that way in the sketch. But instead he found himself modeling Neda's little goat, and wondered at the completed figure—Peter, holy now with simplicity and quietness.

Dobry told himself as an excuse for Peter's being there and nearest to the manger:

"The Child would love an animal, small like Peter, scraggly and with new horns. He would love it!"

When it was all done, Dobry looked at it and called it good. It was a dream he alone had dreamed and brought to life. The dream he had carried for months in his mind and heart had been born, and born alive.

Dobry knelt in the snow but prayed for nothing. He had already emptied his mind and heart. And now without a thought to disturb him, he felt completely one with morning and snow—at peace. Without making any noise, he went upstairs again and, tired out from his work and his feeling, threw himself on the bed in all his clothes and slept.

Grandfather went out, expecting to feed the animals and chickens, and forgot even to question how the work had been done. He took off his sheepskin cap and knelt down before the Nativity. Too forgetful of himself for prayers of asking, he knelt there, aware only of the Holy Child who had come to their home.

Roda called to him from the kitchen, "We need water. More water! Will you haul some right away?" But Grandfather never answered her. He felt that he was drinking wine.

Roda came out to hurry him, but instead of speaking, fell on her knees beside him. They stayed there together, in complete silence, forgetful of time. The Child had come to their home. And neither of them ever before had seen a Nativity like this one. The Greek Orthodox Church has paintings but no sculpture. The Child, Mary, Joseph, and the good animals blessed by the Child had been born of their snow, snow from the village sky, the water that would help create their bread and their wine.

Roda reached out her hand to touch Grandfather. She said, "You are right about Dobry. You are right. God made Dobry an artist and who am I to set my heart against it."

Tidings of the Child spread abroad and not only every peasant in the village came to visit with the Holy Family, but peasants from villages miles away hitched up their buffaloes to sledges and came to pray in the snow. All day long they crowded in, and on Christmas night the courtyard was lighted by their candles and loud with their songs.

Neda came, knelt before the Nativity, and Dobry ran out to kneel beside her. Neither of them spoke, yet they said more to each other than ever before. As they came into the house Dobry whispered to Neda and his voice made her tremble.

"You are my Mary," Dobry said.

BETWEEN Christmas and New Year, Grandfather was busy in a secret way, because Bulgarians give New Year presents instead of Christmas presents. Grandfather was busy especially, because in Bulgaria a peasant gives presents at New Year to those only who are younger than himself and naturally Grandfather's age made him the busiest and most secretive person in the whole village.

He looked over all his sashes, trying to make up his mind about which one Dobry would like best. At last he decided on a sash wider, longer even than the others and handwoven in green with a pattern of storks.

"It looks like April," Grandfather told himself.

He sorted out ancient Greek, Macedonian, and Turkish

coins their family plow had turned up through the years and made two bracelets out of the coins, one for Roda and the other for Neda. Bracelets as strong as they were beautiful, the coins linked together by wrought iron links Pinu let him make in the blacksmith shop.

Remembering that Hristu had made him a pair of birthday shoes, Grandfather whittled a flute out of river linden and painted it with autumn colors for the shoemaker. And once started on flute making, he made up his mind to give Michaelacky, Semo, and Pinu each a new painted flute. But Grandfather could think of nothing for Asan, and he said to Roda:

"I can't think of a present for that narrow-faced, half-asleep boy. Nothing! If I could give him a flute now—but he already has the most wonderful flute anybody ever saw."

Roda relieved his mind and his curiosity, too, by showing him a blouse she had woven for Asan and a golden-looking dress she had woven for Neda, because the two of them were without their mothers.

Dobry, too, was busy. He carved out a wooden lamb for Semo's baby, who was able to walk now. For Neda he made two fantastic slender animals out of the very hard wood of their mountain dran bush.

Dobry felt he had to make these animals out of dranwood, because the dran bush always begins its budding under snow in time for New Year's Eve, and a budding dran branch had come to mean New Year itself. First to leaf out under late snow and last to ripen its cranberry-like fruits, early snow often covered the dranka berries so that the dran bush was looked upon as the spirit of the year, alive to each season and friendly with snow.

On New Year's Eve everybody in the village carried dran branches, as a hint to winter that even the heartiest welcome may be worn out. These branches of sheathed buds were the image of spring. And eager for spring itself, the peasants now turned their backs on winter and were expecting spring to come faster than was possible in a high mountain village such as theirs.

Every peasant looked forward now to his bath as well as to spring's coming. The gypsies brought their massaging bear along in early spring, and if the bear would take his bath in the Yantra river then the villagers knew that the water was warm enough for themselves and they could wash and soak in the river without any fear of cramps.

Roda killed the oldest rooster in their courtyard for New Year's Eve. Only the oldest rooster was thought wise enough to predict the details of spring's arrival, and Roda had invited Semo, his peasant wife, and walking baby to a Weather-man Rooster supper.

And for the first time in his life, Dobry felt impatient of holiday ceremony, eager to be off to Neda with his fantastic animals and a story he had made up to go with them, a part of his New Year present to her.

But Na lay took possession of him when twilight took possession of the earth. Semo's walking baby came in at twilight, switched everybody with a dran branch, and said as best he could:

"Surva, Surva, survaknetca godina," or Happy New Year, a greeting all Bulgarians call out to each other. And a Bulgarian is allowed to switch anybody older than himself when he chants the New Year greeting.

Dobry no sooner thought of Na lay than he began to sing it at the top of his lungs. Everybody sang the gypsy song with him and when it was done Roda took up a dran branch, a candle, and a little pot of incense. And Semo's baby, being the youngest of them all, followed her on a small pilgrimage about the house while Roda blessed each room in preparation for the New Year.

The others were very quiet at table, waiting. Roda came back, set the candle in the middle of the table, lifted the boy to his stool, and for a moment everybody felt too excited to speak, anticipating the pause and death of one year before another year leaps to take its place.

Grandfather took up a dran branch, held it over the candle, said, "Roda, this is your branch!" And Roda, anxiously watching, knew her luck by the number of leaf buds the flame popped open. There were three buds on Roda's branch, two of them popped, but if only one had opened, Roda would have expected little from this New Year. If no buds at all had opened, Roda would have expected the year ahead to be a waste year.

Grandfather said, "Well, two is fairly good. If three leaf buds had opened the year would have belonged to you, Roda. Now you will have to belong a little to this New Year."

He told everybody's fortune by holding a dran branch over the candle and then carved up the weather-wise rooster, saving out the wishbone for himself.

"I keep the weather man for myself," he said. "Why not? I see through him better than any of you do."

And his rooster meat eaten, Grandfather held its wishbone up to the candle flame, shut one eye, peered through the bone.

"Very clear. No snow. No clouds even," he declared. "Perfect! An early spring this year. The earliest spring I ever saw in a weather bone. All of the bone transparent. Perfect! Yes, the gypsy bear will be here before long and we'll take our baths! You'll see me rolling in the river like a buffalo. The water will be high this year, but I'll soak up a lot of river. And how we'll all feel after our baths! Perfect!" Grandfather made a big noise of snorting as if he already felt himself a water buffalo.

Dobry got up to go to Neda but Semo stopped him. "Wait a minute," Semo begged him. "I have to tell you about your New Year present. It's—well, your Nativity made me think of it, Dobry. I'm going to give you that little north room in the school and let you work there with your clay. An hour out of school time every day. Then——"

Roda interrupted the schoolmaster. "Wait, wait!" she cried to Dobry, gathered up the fortune-telling dran branches, putting them away carefully on a shelf under the jamal's hood to be the family's survaktcy for the coming year. The survaktcy is used when anybody hesitates about getting up at daybreak. An earlier riser beats a tattoo with dran branch on the lazy one's bed, repeats, "Surva, surva, survaknetca godina!" until the laziest person in the world would rather get up than listen to the tiresome racket.

"Come here!" Roda called to Dobry and took out from her pocket a handful of gold coins. "The coins from my wedding dress," she told him. "I saved them for you, all of them. Coins from the head kerchief, coins from all around the hem of the skirt. They're for you—" Roda made her voice steadier. "They're for you so you can go to Sofia and grow to be an artist." Grandfather shook his head gravely. "You go in the spring, Dobry, after you've had your bath," he said. "I've saved all the money we got from the wood for your art education. That's a New Year present for you, too."

DOBRY waited longer at home on New Year's Eve than he had intended. Time was as swift as his response to generosity while he dreamed and talked things over in a measured way with Grandfather, his mother, and Semo. And before leaving he had to get into his new sash, Grandfather holding one end while Dobry twirled about. It was late, the last hour of the old year, when he got to the shoemaker's house.

Neda sat under the jamal's hood in the golden-looking dress Roda had woven for her New Year, and listened to her father playing a shoemaker's tune on his new painted flute. Hristu hummed bits of the song as he played, now and then singing a few words and repeating the first verse, because he knew all the words of that:

> "Leather, leather, leather, leather,
> Hairless hide for every weather.
> Cut it, bind it, turn the soles
> And people walk it full of holes.
> Leather, leather, leather, leather."

Hristu's spectacles, the firelight on them, flashed a welcome and when he was done with the song, Neda jumped up, switched Dobry with a dran branch, and laughed out:

"Surva, Surva, survaknecta godina!"

"I brought you two animals," Dobry told her, and greeted Hristu with his eyes. "Look! Carved out of dranwood."

"Animals?" Hristu asked. "But what animals? I never saw any animals like those two. They'd be too skinny for pigs, too tall for goats, and God Himself knows that they can't be oxen or water buffaloes," and Hristu opened his eyes wide enough to fit his spectacle rims.

"But I love them," Neda said. "They're beautiful animals. Beautiful! What are they, Dobry? What animals? They don't look a bit like any of the animals we learn about in school. They don't look like elephants. They aren't giraffes or tigers or panthers."

"Why should they be?" Dobry asked her. "These are the two animals Noah forgot and I made up a story to go with them."

Hristu put his flute up on the jamal's shelf and said, "Well, if you made up a story. Go ahead. Tell it to us.

We have nothing to do but wait for this New Year. Go ahead—tell it!"

Dobry got himself a stool, pulled it up to the jamal, and told them the story.

The Two Animals Noah Forgot

Noah took the Wickerwockoffs as a matter of course. He had watched Wickerwockoffs grow up, watered, fed them, and taught Wickerwockoffs to mind the goats and sheep. So had Mother Noah. And so had Shem, Ham, and Japheth.

But the Wickerwockoff was a peculiar, beautiful animal. Useful in a way that ought to surprise you. And his bones, a leaf-like design of bones showed up under his fine hair and skin.

Mother Noah often said to the three boys, Shem, Ham, and Japheth, "Even as babies your skin and hair were not so fine as that of a Wickerwockoff. The hair and the skin of a Wickerwockoff is as fine as the hair and the skin of a leaf."

And besides the leaf-like design of their bones, the Wickerwockoffs had curving necks, pointed heads with pointed noses, long legs, and short tails—something like deer tails. The male Wickerwockoff was a light brown. The female Wickerwockoff was a lighter brown by two or three shades.

But unlike their friends, the deer, these Wickerwockoffs lived on flies, all kinds of flies, including the heel fly, all kinds of ants, including the blackest ants; on cutworms, mosquitoes, fleas, locusts, beetles, weevils, and on all kinds of ticks, including the sheep tick.

"Very sensible of them," Mother Noah told everybody.

But Noah himself and the three boys, Shem, Ham, and Japheth, loved the Wickerwockoffs for other reasons.

"The Wickerwockoff," you would hear them say, "is beautiful, isn't it? Never stupid. And shy as a twilight is shy."

Shem and Ham and Japheth each had a Wickerwockoff. Shem called his Wickerwockoff, Mahalaleel. Ham called his Wickerwockoff, Sari. Mahalaleel was light brown, but Sari was a lighter brown by two or three shades. And Japheth hoped to have a Wickerwockoff, whose father would be Mahalaleel and whose mother would be Sari. Japheth thought of calling his Wickerwockoff, Little Enos.

The three boys took care of their father's herds with the help of Mahalaleel and Sari. The sheep bleated and the cattle lowed, but the Wickerwockoffs made no sound for themselves—never murmured the way other beasts do. And Shem, Ham, and Japheth could ease themselves on a hillside, put their minds on anything they wished while Mahalaleel and Sari watched the herds of sheep and goats below them. When the nights grow longer and the boys had to shut their eyes against the brightness of a star or the smoke from the camp fire, Mahalaleel and Sari watched for them, lying close to their feet.

And then one day clouds began coming into the sky. A few at a time came in. Then more and more clouds began coming in until the sky itself was nothing but a cloud. A whole cloud! Whereupon it rained, as you know. Not a rainless minute for forty days and forty nights.

But Noah had his Ark ready, built out of gopher wood

and covered inside and outside with pitch. A boat three stories high with doors and windows. And Noah meant to take two of every living thing into the Ark with him and his family and the food necessary for each one.

"First the Wickerwockoffs," said Noah. "We must get plenty of food together for them."

"Yes, first the Wickerwockoffs," said Shem, Ham and Japheth.

"H'mm. Not easy to do," said Mother Noah, "not in this flood. The water comes up and up. And the herds of Wickerwockoffs have already eaten the best of the flies, including the heel flies; the best of the ants, including the blackest ants; the best of the mosquitoes, fleas, cutworms, beetles, weevils, and all kinds of ticks, including the sheep ticks."

"Still we must find all we can," said Noah. "We must have food enough for the Wickerwockoffs. It may be days and days, may be weeks and weeks, months even before the waters dry."

"We must have plenty of food for the Wickerwockoffs," said Shem, Ham, and Japheth.

And Mother Noah, being a peace-loving woman, said no more.

It was very tiring work, difficult, exciting work—the deep water moved and the rain still came. But Father Noah and his three boys labored all night and all day getting ants and locusts down from the trees or out of the bark, flies down from the ceilings and jamal chimneys, enough worms up from the earth, digging here, digging there. They stood waist-deep in moving water, digging everywhere. After that they had to scoop mosquito wrigglers up from the bottoms of old wells and rain barrels. It took them days and days, nights and nights of digging and scooping. The water came up and up and Mother Noah got more impatient to be off on the Ark. But Noah and the three boys, Shem, Ham, and Japheth, still worked away getting food enough together for the Wicker-wockoffs.

"They eat little enough," said Shem.

"I'd hate to see them go hungry," said Ham.

"Oh, they mustn't go hungry," said Japheth.

"I think we have food enough for them now," said Noah. "I'm tired out. We are all tired out."

And Noah was right. They were all tired out. The water came and came and there were innumerable birds and beasts to be caught up and the food for each to be thought on. And Mother Noah was getting more impatient to be off on the Ark! Everybody went around saying:

"Are the storks aboard?"

"Where are the nightingales?"

"Have we food enough for the buffaloes?"

"Couldn't we possibly get smaller oxen?"

"Why do we have to take skunks? And there's no sense to giraffes having all this neck!" Finally Father Noah, tired as he was tired and distracted as he was distracted, shouted out:

"All aboard who's going aboard!"

"I just clutched a bundle of clothes and a bundle of bread and went," Mother Noah said, when she told about it afterward.

All of them were busy—Father Noah and Mother Noah, Shem, Ham, and Japheth—busy managing the Ark, busy caring for innumerable animals and birds with difficult customs, habits and ideas. It was more than a week before anybody thought about Mahalaleel and Sari.

"Why the devil! We thought they were with you," Shem told his father.

"They weren't my Wickerwockoffs," Noah said, but his voice had trouble in it. "Belonged, didn't they, to you three boys? What would I be doing with them? They must be around somewhere. Ask your mother where they are."

But Mother Noah felt certain. The moment Shem asked her, "Where are the Wickerwockoffs?"—she felt positive no Wickerwockoffs were aboard.

"Both the dogs have fleas," she said, as if speaking to herself. "The bread has weevils and—" But Noah interrupted, his head and enormous beard came up above the hatchway.

"Carpenter ants are working on the knee timbers in the hold," he informed her.

Mother Noah paid no attention to him. The mosquitoes were too many for her. She clapped her hands, tried to catch one but of course she couldn't.

"Flies and ants are eating our honey, Mother!" Noah called up the hatchway.

But Shem, Ham, and Japheth didn't care. "How could we have forgotten Mahalaleel and Sari?" they asked each other.

"We were all tired out," Father Noah tried to comfort them. "The water came and came and there were innumerable birds and beasts to be caught up and the food for each to be thought on. And there the Wickerwockoffs were! Nobody dreamed that *they* could be left behind!"

"It was too easy to take them." Mother Noah lamented. "So easy to take them that we forgot them altogether."

When the waters began to dry, Noah opened all the windows of the Ark. "There!" He panted to take in air. And before long the Noahs were walking good earth again, walking down from Mount Ararat. The beasts came behind, the birds flew overhead. And with them, all kinds of flies, including the heel fly, came down from Mount Ararat; all kinds of ants, including the blackest ants; mosquitoes, fleas, cutworms, locusts, weevils, beetles, and all kinds of ticks, including the sheep tick. Only the Wickerwockoffs were missing.

Neda laughed up at Dobry, touched his hand but said nothing. Hristu stared at the two animals Dobry had carved out of dranwood and exclaimed:

"So that's what they are—Wickerwockoffs. The two animals Noah forgot. I wish he'd kept his head."

Neda said, "We'll put them up on the jamal, Dobry, and all the children ever born in this house will hear the story about the two animals Noah forgot. Every child will ask about them—'What animals are those?' And centuries and centuries from now, grandfathers will be telling the story."

Hristu hurried off to get wine, so that he and Neda and Dobry could drink the New Year in. Neda got up, followed him out and came back in a minute with a New Year loaf she had baked. "The Bugavitca loaf," she said, "and fresh from the oven."

Dobry took six tomatoes out of the new sash Grandfather had given him. "These were cold from the snow," he said, "but they don't feel exactly cold now. They'll taste good with your bread, though."

And because the bread was a Bugavitca loaf, the first bite each one of them took was not eaten but saved to put under their pillows that night to dream on and perhaps learn what this New Year might be up to.

The village church bells shook their heads. Yes, New Year! New Year! And after he had drunk the New Year in with a mug of wine, Hristu went to bed to sleep on his piece of Bugavitca bread, and Dobry and Neda sat on under the jamal's hood.

"Guess what?" Dobry asked her. "For one thing, Semo is giving me that little north school room to keep my clay in and work. But—you never could guess this. I can't believe it yet myself. In the spring after we all have our baths, I'm going to study at the art school in Sofia, Neda. Think of that!"

Neda closed her tell-tale eyes. "If you go away off to Sofia, you may never come back," she said.

"Me!" Dobry cried. That's the only thing I feel certain about—coming back. First, I'll have to come back some autumn for a betrothal feast and then I'll have to come back again in either January or February, because everybody is married in one of those two months. You know that, Neda. You know because you look different now—unfolded, beautiful! Like the dran bush when its leaves open out naturally and not over a candle. All new!"

THE weather turned clear as the weather-bone had predicted, a blue sky over deathly cold and snow. And on New Year's Day Maestro Kolu surprised Dobry by sending him a cap of white astrakhan.

"I have my cap from Macedonia," Dobry told everybody. "White astrakhan and you see my hair now—very black."

He wore the cap to school and all the peasants understood that it was a cap nobody would wish to take off. But Dobry explained to Semo, "It does something wonderful to me, so I keep my cap on, school or no school."

When Semo dropped into the little north room to talk

to him, Dobry was working away at an enormous lump of clay, the astrakhan cap still on his head.

"What are you making?" Semo asked him. "I wished to talk to you before you set to work. I am troubled about you, Dobry. Look, your grandfather and your mother think that a little sum from wood chopped and hauled and a handful of wedding coins will put you through art school in Sofia. They won't. Your mother and your grandfather think that life in Sofia is exactly like life in this village. It isn't."

Dobry cocked his white astrakhan cap over one ear and his eyes went brilliant with laughter.

"But what is that to worry about—coins! Every Mama in the village has a wedding dress heavy with coins. If I need more—all right, but don't worry about it. The village is full of coins. Who cares?"

"But—" Semo began earnestly.

Dobry interrupted him, "If I need more coins I'll have them—that's all. A week from today I'll have plenty of coins, anyway. This year I dive for the golden cross on the feast of Saint John the Baptist. In this cold nobody else wishes to take the risk. There's no question about who will bring up the cross this year. I dive by myself. Michaelacky has forbidden his son—the Little Mayor—to dive and every old Mama in the village is going around saying that if any boy goes down into the ice hole this year, he will come up an icicle. But Grandfather says that if no boy dives for the cross on this feast of Saint John the Baptist, it will be a lasting shame for the village. And its men to come will be unfit masters for our oxen and our water buffaloes. This coldest winter makes the dive more important—that's all." Semo got himself a little bench and sat down.

"On the feast of Saint John the Baptist, I take off my white astrakhan cap, Semo, and you will see me dive into the ice hole. And there'll be so many gold coins tossed into my crucifix basket that I'll be able to take some to your brother's family in Sofia when I go there—a present from the village. Mountain coins on your niece's wedding dress, Semo, and she will bear strong sons. Very strong sons with deep roots." Dobry shook his head. And Semo went back to his teaching, feeling somehow that his brother's family in Sofia were about to come into their own.

On the seventh of February, the feast of Saint John the Baptist, the village priest bundled himself up and then got into his stiff robes, put on his tall black hat, took his crozier, a golden crucifix, and set off for the Yantra River. Altar boys and a peasants' choir followed him with incense and chants. Ruddy-faced children got in their way, but looked up with eyes bright and trustful enough to avert scoldings.

Peasant men, Grandfather at their head, broke a big hole in the river ice with iron poles and stood to look at the water underneath, black, powerful, deep moving. The village priest threw the golden crucifix into the water. Dobry dived in and was out again so quickly with the cross that the crowding peasants had only time to think, as they all did think, "The Boy who made our Nativity!" and hold their breath in suspense.

Their tension broke loose in a happy roar that drowned all prayers and chants. And a ceremony that was usually very quiet turned into an uproar. Peasants shouted to each other, "The boy who made our Nativity!" "Nobody else would risk it!" "This cold is like death cold!" "He did it, you saw him?" "Is he all right?" "Fine, fine!" "All of him glows! The skin very red." "Everybody—even the Mayor said it was impossible this year—impossible!" Other peasants roared without words, opened their mouths to let their emotion out.

And the villagers had always singled out the boy who came up with the crucifix as a boy in another country might be singled out for a scholarship. Each winter the villagers put what money they had into the basket holding the wet cross, a lift toward the boy's grown up life, so that he might buy himself a pig or a cow or even a small field.

Dobry, dry, glowing, got into fleece-lined sheepskins, put on his white astrakhan cap, placed the golden crucifix in its basket.

The basket was immediately filled up with golden coins old Mamas had ripped from their wedding dresses and multiplied by the coins the men brought along in their sashes.

Grandfather, Roda, Semo, Hristu, all tried to embrace Dobry at once, so that Neda could only shiver and call up to him:

"It must have been terrible—that water?"

Dobry looked down into her eyes while the others embraced him, and said to her:

"But I'm warm now, Neda. Na lay. And the dive was more important this year." He disentangled himself from the crowd and ran headlong for home.

And that night everybody in the village danced the rachanitza. Old Mamas, grandfathers, children, everybody danced. Dobry and Neda and Roda and Grandfather danced at the mayor's house with a crowd of peasants, Asan playing the music for them on his wonderful flute.

WINTER, for all its cold, was shorter than usual and spring came with a rush of green water and green leaves. An eager spring in the mountains, wild grass pushed up through pine needles, while sunless mountainsides were still patched with snow. The poplar tree in Dobry's courtyard had leaves again and the leaves were big and mature for their age.

Every peasant had danced himself into perspiration during the wedding months of January and February. And salty wet now behind his plow, the peasant felt that the Gypsy Bear was his most urgent necessity.

Villagers exclaimed, "But the bear should be here! Those gypsies—to the devil with them! Nobody can depend on them. The river might be warm enough now for a soap bath and a swim."

Yet no peasant took off his winter clothes to soak himself clean in the high, rip-roaring Yantra until the Gypsy Bear came to prove by going in that the water was as warm as it should be and the spring current less powerful than it looked. It was a matter of tradition, custom, and commonsense that waited upon the Gypsy Bear.

Bears love to wash up in spring and the Gypsy Bear was as reliable as a thermometer. Water he found comfortable, uncramping and a current that he could master always proved to be equally comfortable, uncramping and safe for the peasants.

The gypsies followed spring up the mountains, stopping over at every village with their massaging and bath-testing bear. They stayed on at each village, tempted by peasant food, tempted by peasant dancing and the love they had for fiddling out the song everybody sang:

"Spring is flighty,
Highty-tighty.
Love is fresher than the grass,
Life is lighter, nights are whiter,
With the sky a petaled mass.

"Spring is flighty,
Highty-tighty.
Hills of snow run warm, run free.
Sun is throbbing, quail go bobbing
Under dran bush, under tree.

"Love is flighty,
Highty-tighty,
Sudden as a waterfall.
Bees are fatter. What's the matter?
Clap her now or not at all!"

Dobry waited for the Gypsy Bear with a special kind of excitement, because he was going to leave for Sofia on the morning after his bath. The adventure of uprooting himself from the village made Dobry feel that all of life was too uncertain for caution. And, impatient for the swim, he plunged into the Yantra river when the bear plunged in. Dobry swam with the bear and loafed with him in the water, content to feel himself a bear instead of the water buffalo Grandfather liked to imagine himself when taking his spring bath.

Every villager went into the Yantra for a swim and a scrub with homemade soap, while gypsies ate, drank, fiddled, and danced on the river bank. Grandfather said, "It may look like spring but it never feels like spring until we get into the river." And he drove Hristu's water buffaloes down to the Yantra to get their spring baths while other peasants danced the Horo in the village square.

Woodpeckers, yellow hammers, nightingales, woodcrows, all of them were back in mountain trees. Only the village storks had not come and their absence intensified Dobry's feeling that all of life was moving in a new direction.

Grandfather was to drive Dobry as far as the mill town in the morning and see him off for Sofia. And after taking the buffaloes to the river, Grandfather busied himself in the courtyard, washing down Sari and Pernik before combing them out, polishing their horns, and greasing their hoofs. Dobry found him at work there and offered to help. Grandfather looked up from his scrubbing: "What the devil?" he cried. "You just had your bath and you must keep yourself clean for the trip tomorrow. All the soap in the village is used up and you and I have to be off before daybreak. And I love it—but love it—to get oxen ready for a journey." He went on, excitedly scrubbing Pernik's flank.

Dobry left him, went into the kitchen and took a stool. His mother was kneading bread. She kneaded and perspired, kneaded and perspired, her long braids pinned back out of the way. She said to him:

"I'll make an enormous ring of bread. You can carry it on your arm. I'll put the cheese bread in your basket with the other things. I have everything on my mind today. Besides all the special cooking for your baskets, I must get around to washing everything up fresh for your bundles. There's so little time left now. We all stayed too long in the river."

"I'll haul the water," Dobry said and got up.

"You! You must do nothing today except keep yourself clean for the journey," Roda said emphatically and slapped the bread into an enormous circle with her vigorous slaps.

Dobry went out the kitchen door, feeling that he had stopped being Dobry and become only a boy who was leaving the world for a place called Sofia. He felt separated from everything that belonged to his life.

The locust trees were in bloom up and down the village streets. "Locusts in bloom and still no storks!" Dobry thought. He climbed up a steep canyon, hoping to find Asan and the village cows in its top meadow, but instead found a dran bush there, covered with late flowers because of the altitude and crowded around by pine trees. Dobry threw himself on the young wild grass under the dran bush, put his head on its roots, and looked up from its cloud of dran blossoms to a cloud topping a mountain peak.

"Everything is one," he thought. "All the same thing—earth, everything—One. And I'm a part of it all." He thought about Hadutzi-dare and said to himself: "Mountains cannot say No to me. Rivers stop to let me pass, valleys are my servants. The darkest canyon gives me a present."

He lay there until day turned, drawing up strength from the earth.

A whirring, rattling noise startled him. Dobry jumped up, threw his cap to the sky. All the village storks—the mayor's stork, the blacksmith's storks, the coppersmith's storks, the two storks that belonged in Neda's courtyard, his own storks, circled the forest sky and headed down for the village. Dobry broke off heavy dran branches, ran down the mountain alongside a torrent, and burst into the shoemaker's courtyard.

Neda looked up, startled. She was dressed afresh after her river bath in blue cotton, green aproned. And little wet braids shone on her forehead. She was making cakes for Dobry's journey baskets in the courtyard oven and, in her anxiety for the goodness of the little cakes, had made herself too warm by opening the oven doors oftener than was necessary.

"Look! The dran flowers!" Dobry said to her. "We'll get a whole bucketful of dran berries when we have our Betrothal Feast instead of the cupful Mother buys from the gypsies every fall. Where's Peter?"

Neda took the dran branches and tried to smile up at him.

"Peter?" she asked. "I let him go off to feed with Michaelacky's goats today. All the goats were going to fat grass and I——"

"Never mind," Dobry told her. "I'll see him before I go. It never seemed real to me until today. About going away, I mean. Never!"

Neda closed her eyes and could hardly speak. "But when you come back you'll be a great man—a great artist. Your grandfather says you will be and Semo tells me that, too."

"Of course," Dobry shook his head. "That's why I'm going. And that's why I'm coming back, too, Neda. Neda!"